When LOVE Turns To Hate

A NOVEL BY

SHARRON DOYLE

WHERE
HIP HOP
LITERATURE
BEGINS...

AUGUSTUS
PUBLISHING

© 2010 Sharron Doyle
ISBN: 9780982541517

Novel by Sharron Doyle
Edited by Anthony Whyte
Creative Direction & Design by Jason Claiborne
Cover Model: Crystal Lane

Augustus Publishing paperback JUNE 2010
www.augustuspublishing.com

ACKNOWLEDGEMENTS

All praises due to the Most High for delivering me and giving me life on a new journey. I always know that He is there carrying me, watching over me, through the rough times even when I just wanted to give up.

My mother Miss Sheila, who means the world to me, I love and adore you. Jimmy Smith, the man behind the woman, who has proven to be ride or die. I love you babe! Cherie things will get greater later…just hold on. Taikeya keep striving. You make me so proud just keep doing what you're doing. The world is yours and everything in it. Taisheem and Che'la stay educated. I love y'all to death you are the future. Rahsaan come home we're waiting for you. They can't hold you in captivity forever. Aunt Bev thanks for being there through everything. To my girls who have stuck by me through the years and cried tears. Monique Gary, Joyce Copeland, Rachelle Venable, Shasheila Benn… Breathe easy. God got us. Jason Jarvis who's been there from the beginning. Tanya Sebastian, I can't wait for you to come home! You have been down long enough.

To my peeps in Far Rockaway, Jherri Querrard, Nilda Imes, Kristal Middleton, Robin White, Victor 'Smokey' Padilla and Maria, Giselle Calvo, and Eric Coleman. Thanks to Jill Robinson and Dennis Void. To all the authors who have opened doors for me, and made it possible by laying down the path, I am truly grateful. To the readers who have supported me from the beginning when I started this journey in the penile system. Y'all know who you are. Thanks a million. Thanks Tamiko Maldonado, Juliet White and special thanks to Anthony Whyte and Jason Claiborne, the amazing Augustus Manuscript Dream Team, who know how it's done. If they can't do it then… It can't be done! Go hard or go home!

One Love, Sharron Doyle

"HATING PEOPLE IS LIKE BURNING DOWN YOUR OWN HOUSE TO GET RID OF A RAT."

-Harry Emerson Fosdick

CHAPTER ONE
BALTIMORE, MARYLAND

Petie turned over on his side, and put his arm around Patrice's waist. He rubbed her stomach and kissed the back of her neck. Patrice stirred in her sleep lightly and tightened her hand around his. Petie kissed her again and got out of the bed quietly.

He stretched and walked to the window and looked out into his sprawling backyard. The pool always looked inviting in the morning. The red digital numbers on the alarm clock announced that it was six-fifty in the morning. It was almost time for him to wake up Amir.

It had been five years since Petie and Patrice left New York. After arriving in Baltimore, Patrice had given birth to their son, Amir. He was now five years old and the spitting image of his father. The only exception was he had eyes like his mom. Patrice was now seven months pregnant. Petie was excited when Patrice told him that they were having a girl.

When they had arrived in Baltimore, Petie had come clean with Patrice and told her that he was HIV positive. Patrice sat down and cried while Petie admitted that he was sick. It was the hardest thing that Petie had to do. He figured he owed her that much, but Petie never told his wife, Renee.

Petie explained to Patrice that he had been in denial for six years, and that he didn't want to put her through that. Even though the damage was done because it was after the fact, but at least it was out in the open. Patrice told him that she was not going anywhere. She was sticking by him regardless of his condition. She loved him and he was due the same loyalty that he had given her.

She remembered being strung out on crack. Petie took her under his wing and put her back on her feet. She was able to move back down south with her family. Now five years clean, she was happy he helped her take her life back. Petie used to sit with her in Narcotics Anonymous meetings, supporting her. He helped her to realize that she was worthy and that she never had to use crack.

Patrice loved Petie for his dedication to her. Petie wanted the best for Patrice and had showed her that since day one. They were sharing a hotel room when he had told her, "After tonight, no more smoking". Other men were always trying to give her drugs so she could compromise herself for their pleasure. But not Petie, and Patrice was feeling him.

Petie made sure that she ate right, rested, and he even put money in her pocket. The biggest test was when he had left those kilos in the hotel room, not knowing if she would have found them and took off. She didn't. Patrice told Petie that she found it, just in case he knew that it had been touched. She earned his trust and he earned her love. Patrice could not, and would not leave Petie because he was HIV positive. She loved him, ride or die.

Their main concern was Amir's health. They wondered would he be born with the virus and how it would affect him. Petie felt like shit knowing that it was his fault when Amir was born with the virus. Fortunately, Amir's immune system was as healthy as any 5-year-old boy and showed no signs of the virus.

Petie walked down the hall to Amir's room and woke his little boy. 'His champion', he called Amir. Petie kissed Amir's forehead and picked him up out of the bed. The sleepy boy rested his head on his father's shoulder and Petie carried him down the hall into the bathroom. He sat Amir on the toilet seat.

"Do you have to use the bathroom?"

Amir rubbed his eyes and nodded his head. Petie lifted him off the toilet seat and pulled his Batman pajamas down. When Amir was finished relieving himself, Petie told him, "Wipe with the toilet paper." Petie brushed his teeth and held Amir up to the mirror with his own toothbrush so that he could brush his own teeth. Like father, like son.

"Let's go downstairs and make some breakfast," Petie said, picking up his youngest son.

He remembered, carrying Darnell and Donte, his other sons, around until they were too big. No matter what, Petie was a damn good father and no one could take that from him.

Petie cooked turkey bacon, scrambled eggs and English muffins for breakfast. He and Amir ate in the kitchen. Then he made a plate for Patrice. He liked waking her up and serving her breakfast in bed. Her pregnancy was taking a lot of her energy. Patrice was always tired, sleeping all day, only getting up to cook or eat. Petie cooked dinner on several occasions so that she could just rest. He had told her that he did not want her putting any stress on his unborn, his first daughter at that. "Nothing better go wrong," he always said.

"Good morning, baby", she said, sitting up in bed.

Patrice rolled over and smiled when she saw the breakfast tray.

"Are you feeling alright?" Petie asked, adjusting the pillows behind her back.

"Yes, baby", she answered, smiling. Petie touched her on the cheek and told her that he loved her.

"I love you too, Mommy," Amir said, warmly looking at his mother.

"I love you too, both of you. The best men that a girl could want," Patrice smiled.

Petie bent down and kissed her quickly growing, round stomach and said, "Eat, because my daughter is hungry."

He went downstairs to the kitchen and returned with a glass of carrot juice.

"Here, ma," he said, passing the glass to her. "I'm going to go for a swim."

Amir was on his feet. "Daddy I wanna go too," he said.

"No you stay here with mommy and let daddy go for a swim," Petie said.

He had something to do this morning, and wanted to loosen up before he left. Petie swam every morning, after they had breakfast and before hitting the streets. This morning he did not have time to watch Amir while he swam. He had business that required his full attention to take care of. A couple of laps around the pool would get him focused.

He took the cordless telephone off the charger and set it outside by the pool before diving in. The water was exhilarating and was a sure way to get his heart pumping. Petie swam for nearly an hour before getting out. He shook the water off his dreads and dried off with the towel that he kept by the pool. The telephone rang just as Petie was about to reach for it to go in the house. The caller I.D. read one of his partner's numbers.

He knew what the call was about. Last night, he had gotten word that one of his workers had bounced with two ounces of the product. Petie was not happy with niggas running off with his work, and taking money from his family. Everyone knew that was extremely unhealthy to cross Petie.

"Did you find him?" Petie answered on the second ring.

"Yeah", Chaos said. "He's at Josephine's house. He's been there for about two days. Sissy found out where he was, and hollered at me about ten minutes ago," Chaos explained.

"Get the dogs ready. I'll be there in twenty minutes," Petie said and hung up.

There was nothing else to discuss. He went back inside the house. Patrice and Amir were in the kitchen. She was washing the dishes. Petie walked up behind her. Putting his arms around her, he gently rubbed her stomach while kissing the back of her neck. Amir stood and watched the affectionate exchange between them.

"I got to go out and do something," he said, still rubbing her stomach and leaning his head on her shoulder.

"Uh huh," Patrice said, knowing that 'something' meant business.

"I'll be back before you have to go for your appointment," he said.

"Petie, be careful please," she said, wanting to say more.

She knew not to get involved with his business, but that never stopped her from worrying. Patrice knew Petie's gangsta was off the chain, but she still worried. He was still a wanted man from the incident in New York five years ago.

Petie quickly got dressed and left the house. It was time to take care of business. He backed out of the driveway and headed to the shack to meet up with Chaos. In the truck, he called Sissy to find out who was at Josephine's house.

"A bunch of crackheads," Sissy said sarcastically.

"Ahight, have you seen Dave in there?" he asked, turning the corner.

"Yeah…! Petie, you know I wouldn't tell you anything if I didn't know for sure," she said, sounding a bit offended.

"Ahight then," he said, ending the phone call.

CHAPTER TWO
PENNSYLVANIA

Renee clocked-out of her job and quickly walked to the parking lot. She could not wait to get home. Today had been long and she was tired. If she did not have to get Donte from basketball practice, she would go home and jump right into bed. She had been living in Pennsylvania for five years, and for the first time in her life she felt independent. After making the decision to leave Petie and move to PA., Renee had been living a life that was different from the one she had known.

One of the first things Renee did was get into support groups with other women who were HIV positive. She needed to know how to live with the virus, how to cope with the reality of being positive. She needed to know that she was not alone and that others were going through the same thing. Renee needed to have other women to talk to when she felt like giving up and letting the virus win. The groups taught her how to cope and gave her the encouragement she needed to fight.

The next thing she did was started dating but that came after a year and a half. She had met someone nice. He was a single father with two sons. He understood what Renee was going through in regards to being single again. He had been married and never thought he would be single ever again. It was awkward for both of them, but eventually the ice broke and they realized that they had more in common than just a separation.

Cliff had been understanding, and patient, Renee knew that he was the one. The hardest thing Renee had to do was to tell Cliff she was HIV positive. He had a right to know she had a heath issue, as she preferred to call her diagnosis.

Cliff had said, "We'll be okay. There's ways we can protect ourselves."

Renee cried in his arms. Cliff made her feel safe and wanted. Something Renee had not felt in years. Petie had never made her feel wanted. She knew he only stayed because of their sons. She had felt that way with Ladelle but their relationship was top secret and she knew that they could never come out in the open.

Renee pulled into the parking lot in the back of the high school. Donte was still on the court with the other players. She sat down on the bleachers and watched him play, more like rule the court. She was so proud of Donte. He was a mother's prayer. Now eighteen years old, he was focused. He had never given Renee any problems. He never got into drugs or had any troubles with the law.

Darnell on the other hand was just like Petie. He was the splitting image of his father in attitude and behaviors. Darnell was reckless. Since moving to PA., Darnell had several scrapes with the law. She had told him that PA. was nothing like New York, and the laws were much stricter in the Commonwealth state. Darnell did not care. He had been arrested for possession of marijuana, disorderly conduct, loitering and harassment. Renee thought that the transition to PA. would be healthy for them. Darnell never adjusted and Renee knew that he wouldn't.

The only thing that he did right was graduate from high school. Renee did not know how he managed to graduate with his grades. She figured that the school was doing the other students a favor by graduating him, they wanted him out.

Donte was in his last year of high school and was the school's prize player on the basketball team. He was graduating with honors and with a full scholarship to attend Penn State in the fall. Donte had a girlfriend who Renee really liked. Sonya was a senior who Renee thought was perfect for Donte. She was going to attend Temple University that fall. Donte planned on marrying Sonya. He had told his mother that Sonya was the one, when they first met in the ninth grade.

Donte saw Renee sitting there watching him play. He waved, showing off as he always did when his mother watched him play. He spun on two players and scored a lay-up over them. Looking back, he saw Renee smiling and giving him thumbs up.

After a few more minutes of hoops, Donte said good bye to his teammates and walked toward his mother. She got off the bleachers and met him in the middle of the court. Renee hugged her son and looked up at him as he kissed her on the forehead.

"How's my favorite girl?" he asked as they walked to the car, his arm around Renee's shoulder.

"Tired and a little hungry… By the way who's cooking tonight?" she asked before getting in the car. Donte got in on the passenger's seat and said, "We both will. What are we having anyway?"

"I took out some chicken, so we can fry them up and make some cabbage and rice. How does that sound?" Renee said, pulling into traffic.

"Sounds good mom, is Darnell home yet?" Donte asked.

Renee sighed in frustration and said, "Who knows, you know he comes in when he wants to."

Donte didn't say anything. He wished that his older brother would do the right thing. He knew that Darnell put a lot of unwanted pressure on their mother. In a way, he hated Darnell for that. When they were younger, Donte looked up to Darnell as if he was a God. He followed Darnell everywhere and wanted to be just like him. When their parents separated, Darnell became resentful. He became bitter, and became very disrespectful to their mother. Donte could not stand it. Sometimes he wondered if Darnell was smoking something other than weed. He felt like he did not know his brother anymore. They had grown apart, and Donte did not like that either but he refused to follow Darnell anymore. They were a year apart but it seemed like they were worlds apart.

They parked in front of the house and got out. DMX was blaring out the speakers in the living room. Renee opened the door, walked right to the stereo system, and turned the music down. She could smell weed in the air underneath the air freshener Darnell sprayed. She went upstairs to Darnell's room. The door was closed and she turned the knob and pushed the door open. Renee's mouth dropped open. Darnell jumped in surprise.

"What the fuck!" he screamed. He quickly pulled up his pants. "Why didn't you knock on my fucking door!" he yelled looking at Renee with bloodshot eyes.

"Get out!" Renee said to the girl who had Darnell's dick in her mouth. "Right now, get out!"

"Why didn't you knock on my fucking door?" Darnell yelled.

"I don't have to knock! This is my goddamn house. Who the fuck do you think you talking to?" she barked. The girl reached for her pocketbook and got up off the bed.

"I'm sorry, ma'am," she said.

Renee felt embarrassed for the girl. She was not mad at her, only Darnell. He was so much like Petie that it made her stomach turn. Donte stood in the doorway and watched the heated exchange between his mother and his brother. He felt like hitting Darnell.

"Get out my room!" Darnell ordered his mother.

"Get out of your room?" Renee repeated incredulously. This boy must be smoking crack, she thought. "Your room is in my house!"

"This ain't your house. My dad bought this house!" he yelled back at her.

"Stop talking to mommy like that, Darnell. What is wrong with you?" Donte asked as if he was talking to a stranger.

"Mind your fucking business schoolboy. Your name should be Shonte and not Donte. You fucking wuss!" Darnell shouted at his brother.

"Darnell that's enough you better watch your mouth or you can find somewhere else to live," Renee said and walked out the room.

"Good, 'cause I wanna go live with my dad anyway!" Darnell shouted and slammed his door in their faces.

Donte walked down the stairs and went into the kitchen. Renee was leaning against the counter crying. He put his arm around her.

"It's alright mom. Don't cry. Darnell will change. He's just going through something," Donte said, trying to comfort his mother.

The truth was he did not believe that Darnell would ever change.

Renee turned toward her son and said, "Donte, he's been going through something for five years. I'm tired of it. I think he should go down south with, Petie."

She went to the living room, got the telephone off the coffee table, and called Petie. Enough was enough. Renee couldn't take it anymore. Darnell was only getting worse.

"Donte, you season the chicken while I talk to your father," she said.

Donte did as he was told and had the chicken in the pan frying by the time she was off the telephone. Darnell came down the stairs and sat on the sofa. He reached for the remote control and turned the big screen television on. He flipped through the channels, stopped at BET's 106th and Park. Then he turned the volume way up.

"Darnell turn that television down," Renee shouted from inside the kitchen.

Darnell only ignored her.

"Turn off the damn television…now!" she ordered.

He kept watching the video. Renee stomped from the kitchen, took the remote off the coffee table, turned the television off, and went back into the kitchen. Darnell turned the TV back on. She stomped out there again and turned it off. Darnell threw the remote against the wall. It cracked into pieces. Renee stared in disbelief at the fallen cracked pieces on the floor.

"Now nobody can watch the fucking TV!" he yelled, stomping out the house, and slamming the door.

"That's it!" Renee declared. "I want him out of here. Your father is going to call back, because he was busy but I want Darnell out of here this week. He's not doing anything with his life since he got out of school, he hangs out all fucking day doing nothing and I want him out of here!" she yelled.

Donte looked at his mother and noticed that she was shaking. He got scared because she was sick and she could not afford to lose any T-cells because of stress.

"Mom, calm down. Let daddy take care of it. You know he will, just please calm down, mom."

Renee sat down at the dining room table and put her head in her hands. Donte was right; she had to calm down. If Renee let Darnell stress her out anymore, she would end up in a hospital. Petie would take care of this situation.

Darnell always did whatever Petie said, and that made Renee

feel like she was doing something wrong. She felt she was a damn good mother. Petie told her that all the time. When she called Petie he had said, "Ma, I can't talk now, but I'll definitely take care of it when I'm done. Let me call you back."

She knew he would. Petie always kept his word.

CHAPTER THREE
BALTIMORE, MARYLAND

Traveling in separate rides, Petie and Chaos pulled up on Josephine's block. Chaos parked on the side of the house and Petie parked in the back. They met at the front. Chaos had the dogs on thick chain leashes. Petie took the masks off the dogs. He hit them on the nose and hissed at them. Two of the dogs growled deeply, they were ready.

Petie knocked on the door and put his hand over the peephole. He could hear footsteps coming from inside the house and then Josephine's voice called out, "Who is it?"

Petie did not answer. He knocked again, this time harder.

Boom! Boom!

"Who the fuck is it…?"

Chaos kicked the door open and pushed Josephine on the floor. Petie stepped into the house with four angry, mean pitbulls.

"Don't bother getting up, bitch. Next time somebody knocks on your fucking door, open it", Chaos said and kicked Josephine in the mouth.

She grabbed her quickly bleeding face and whimpered, "Petie, I didn't know it was y'all at the door or else I'd have opened it the first time you knocked. I swear I would have. I know not to play with y'all".

Three people sat in the living room holding crack pipes and lighters in their hands. They remained frozen like statues when the door flew open and Josephine hit the floor. Petie looked around the room.

"What room is Dave in?" he asked.

One of the guys sitting on the stained sofa pointed and replied, "Second room on the right hand side."

Petie slipped his hand into his favorite pair of brass knuckles and put his hand in his pocket. Chaos pulled Josephine into the living room by her hair and told her, "Get on the fucking couch with the rest of these crackheads."

"I don't know what she did, but I ain't have nothin' to do wit' it," one of the guys said.

"Shut the fuck up!" Chaos ordered him. "Don't none of y'all muthafuckaz say nothin' to me, ya heard?" Everybody shook their heads like first graders. They saw the menacing look Chaos wore. He was not to be played with. He had a cold heart. He did not care about kids, grandmothers, aunts; anyone could get it. Chaos knew no boundaries.

Petie walked down the hall and stopped at the second bedroom door. He listened, turned the knob and found Dave asleep in the bed. Petie let the dogs loose, walked to the bed, and slapped Dave. He jumped up. The dogs started barking. Petie saw the surprise on Dave's face.

"Where's my money at dick?"

"I –I- I- got it, Petie," Dave said, stuttering and reaching into his pocket.

He pulled out eighty-five dollars. With trembling hand, he passed it to Petie.

"I'll get the rest. I swear I will. My girl gets paid on Friday and I'll have it then."

Petie punched him in the face with the brass knuckles, splitting Dave's eye. He screamed, clutching his badly bleeding eye. Petie hit him again. His dogs barked and growled louder waiting to jump on Dave.

"Petie man please, I'll get your money. I swear I will," Dave begged, trying to stop the blood leaking but at this point it was futile.

"I don't want the money. You took my material, bounced, didn't answer your cellphone and then you hid out for four fucking days and now you wanna give me cheddar? You already know what it is, Dave. I told you when I put you on in the beginning 'don't ever steal from my family.' When a nigga take off with my shit it's like they stealing from my son and my girl and I don't play that," Petie calmly explained.

"Petie please man… I'll get your money. Let me tell you what happened…" Dave cried.

Petie hit him again. "Stop trying to play me dick. I already know what happened. You smoked up my shit"!

"No, no I didn't man. Honest to God I didn't," Dave said.

Petie looked at him as if he was stupid. He knew that Dave was smoking.

"Why niggas always try to act as if they don't be hitting the pipe, when they got all the signs? I see your dark hands, sucked in jaw, mouth always moving, clothes dirty, and that makes it evident. Empty out your pockets," Petie ordered, figuring Dave would have a pipe in it.

"I gave you all the money," Dave said.

"Empty out your fucking pockets, dick!" Petie barked at him.

Dave sat up slowly in the bed knowing that if he moved to quickly one of the dogs would jump on him. He emptied his pockets and there it was. A crack pipe loaded with residue. Petie took the pipe and threw it against the wall.

"That's where my material went?"

Dave didn't have a chance to answer. Petie let the dogs

loose and they jumped on him, tearing at his flesh. Dave screamed and hollered in tormenting pain as four pit bulls locked their jaws and pulled his flesh apart. Dave fell on the floor trying to get away. The dogs tore at his throat and stomach. Dave screamed, all the while trying to get the dogs off. There was no getting their jaws off his flesh. Blood splattered on the floor as the dogs attacked Dave. Finally, his body shook with convulsions until he stopped moving. Petie called the dogs off Dave's chewed and torn up body.

His dogs followed him back into the living room. Their paws left bloody prints down the hall. Josephine was on the sofa crying, holding her head and rocking back and forth. The others sat wide eyed and scared to death. They didn't know what was going to happen next.

"Go by the door," Petie ordered the dogs.

Obediently, they went and sat down licking blood off each other's faces.

"Josephine, come here," Petie said.

She got up slowly, and walked over to him on shaky legs.

"Yes Petie. Please don't hurt me. I swear I did not know that nigga had taken off with your shit."

"You lying before I even ask you the question? Shut up!" he said, looking her up and down.

Petie was grilling Josephine, contemplating what to do with her. She let Dave hide out in her crib, she should get it too. Josephine had to know that he was ducking them. His thoughts were stirred by the memory of Patrice. She was a crackhead when they first met, but she was not grimey. She only did what she had to do to get by. Petie felt a soft spot for Josephine.

"Forget I was here. You heard?" he said in a warning tone.

"I will Petie. I swear I will, I don't know nothing," she said, nodding her head quickly and wiping her tears.

"What's my name?" Petie asked staring at her like he was seeing through her.

"I don't know. I never seen you before in my life," she responded.

"Good answer."

Petie nodded at Chaos and opened the door to let his blood stained dogs out. They left as smooth as they came. Outside Petie told Chaos to spray the dogs down and get the clean up boys to get rid of Dave's body. He got in his black Hummer and headed home. He had to take Patrice to the doctor for her sonogram. Petie went to all of her appointments with her the same way he did for Renee. The main thing on his mind was the telephone call from Renee. He had to call back not to speak with her, but to Darnell, his oldest son.

CHAPTER FOUR
NEW YORK CITY

Ladelle closed out the books and went back upstairs. Lydia was waiting for him so they could close up their restaurant and go pick up Ladir, their 5-year-old son.

Five years ago Petie had given Ladelle fifty-thousand dollars before he fled down south. Ladelle had flipped the money a few times, and opened a restaurant. He named it after his first son, Ladir. He and Lydia had gotten married and were doing well. Their restaurant had a dining area, lounge and bar. The club featured ladies' night on Tuesdays, couples' night on Wednesdays, and live jazz for Saturday night enterainment. Lydia felt they should discontinue the Hip-Hop set on Friday nights, because of a younger, rowdy crowd it attracted. She saw trouble coming and would always say, "One of these nights these niggas is gonna act up and tear our club up." Ladelle would tell her not to worry about that because they had extra on those nights.

They drove to his mother's house to pick up Ladir. Ladelle double parked while Lydia went upstairs to get him. Ladelle rubbed his temples and reclined in his seat. Running a restaurant was harder than Ladelle had ever imagined, but it was all worth it. Every time he looked at his son, the long hours at work made it all worthwhile. Ladelle was determined to create a better life for Ladir, one that was easier than he had. Lydia was very business minded. She took care of the books and kept up with the inventory. She was the memory in the team.

Their relationship had become strained in the past year because of running the restaurant and being parents. They were going to Ladir's PTA meeting at school and didn't miss any of his soccer games. There was no private time together, intimate time or even time to make love. Sexually Ladelle had lost interest in Lydia, but he never told her. She had become more of a business partner to him. He didn't know when or why it happened but it did. She was still attractive, just not appealing. Ladelle did not know why but he remembered when Darnell and Donte were born, and Petie had told him that he really did not want to fuck Renee anymore. Now Ladelle understood what Petie was trying to tell him.

Lydia and Ladir came out the building, and got in the car. Ladelle buckled his son's seatbelt, got back into the car and then turned onto 8th Avenue headed to the expressway so they could go home to their posh Central Park West apartment.

"How was school today?" Ladelle asked.

"It was good dad. I got an 'A' on my spelling test, and my teacher wrote 'excellent' on it," Ladir answered, while looking at his father's reflection in the rearview mirror.

"That's because you are excellent," Ladelle said.

"I know dad," Ladir said smiling.

Ladelle winked at his pride and joy and drove carefully on the crowded freeway. He was always more cautious when Ladir was in the car. Now he could appreciate the joy that Petie felt when his sons were born. It was an unexplainable feeling of joy, and love deeper than any ocean. Ladelle felt this way every time he looked at Ladir. Nothing would matter to Ladelle without Ladir.

They pulled up in front of their apartment building. Lydia and Ladir got out. The doorman hurriedly opened the door for them.

"Good evening," he greeted.

"Thank you, Howard," Lydia smiled, stepping into the carpeted lobby.

Ladelle parked the car and went into his building. They rode the elevator upstairs to their beautifully furnished apartment. Ladelle checked the mail that the cleaning lady left on the foyer. Lydia went to their bedroom and started undressing. Her cellphone rang. She retrieved it from of her Coach handbag. Lydia recognized the number on the blue screen and she answered immediately.

"I can't talk now. I'm at home."

"When will I see you?" the caller asked. Lydia looked behind her nervously hoping that Ladelle was not in earshot before continuing. "Tomorrow night after I close up... I gotta go," she said hanging up abruptly.

She could hear Ladelle telling Ladir to get ready for bed.

"Okay dad," Ladir said and went to his room.

Lydia turned the water on in the bathroom and let the heat steam up the bathroom. She could not wait to get underneath the water. Ladelle sat at his desk and sorted the mail, opening bills and more bills. The more money you make, the quicker the bills accumulate, he scratched his head thinking. He pulled out all the ones that had to be addressed immediately. He put the others away and went to the bedroom. Lydia was still in the shower singing. He undressed and propped up the pillows before getting in the bed. Thank God for another successful day, Ladelle whispered when his head hit the pillow.

Lydia came out the shower and sat in front of her vanity mirror. She rubbed White Diamonds lotion on her legs while seductively looking at Ladelle. He reached into the drawer next to the bed and took out a magazine. Lydia stood up in front of him and rubbed the nipples of her 34C's between her fingers. They were taut and so ready. Ladelle glanced up at her.

"Honey, put something on before you catch a cold," he said.

The disappointment was evident on her face. Ladelle just

was not interested in making love to her anymore. Lydia got in the bed and rolled on her side. She had tears in her eyes as she watched Ladelle getting out of bed a short while later.

He left to check on his son who was already in the bed, reading. Ladelle took the book from him and started reading it to him. This is what mattered to him, being there for his son. Before long, he could see Ladir's eyes getting heavy. He knew that any minute he would be fast asleep. Ladelle read a few more lines and looked over at Ladir, only to find him asleep. He read until the book was finished and quietly crept out of the bed exiting the room. Ladelle closed the door behind him and went into the bedroom. Lydia moved away from him when he got in the bed.

"Good night, baby," Ladelle said.

"Yeah, good night," she responded curtly.

CHAPTER FIVE
NEW YORK

Venus parked the car and rushed inside of her first floor apartment she rented in the Bronx. The apartment was located in the house Share owned. She was running late again. Venus and Andre had been together for almost two years, and he had turned out to be a nightmare. Andre was perfect in the beginning of their relationship, but when he moved in with her, he showed his true colors. He was very possessive, strict, and he did not have a problem enforcing his rules. He would deliver a punch here and a smack there. Venus had tried to end the relationship several times, but Andre would have none of that.

Now she checked the time and winced knowing that he would be home in less than and hour. She slipped out of her Donna Karan suit and panty hose and put on something more comfortable. Bullet and Diamond were waiting in the kitchen to eat while she slipped on her housedress. Everyone had his or her demands, even the dogs. Venus poured dog food into their bowls and gave them fresh water.

She opened the refrigerator and took out the hamburger meat, onions, green pepper, and fresh garlic. Venus put on a pot of boiling water for the noodles and checked her watch to see how much time she had left because dinner could not be late. Andre would have a fit. She chopped up the onions, green peppers and garlic. Making sure they were not too big, Andre hated chunks. He wanted everything diced up fine. Venus put the meat into the frying pan and seasoned it, adding the diced up produce. She put some black pepper and then covered it so it could simmer. She opened a box of spaghetti noodles and broke them in half before putting them into the pot of boiling water. In another pot, she started the sauce and seasoned that lightly with oregano.

She went back to the bedroom to hang up her suit and make sure that the room was in order. She did everything she could to keep the peace in her relationship, although she did not know how much longer she could put up with Andre. Some days she loved him to death and other days she hated the sight of him.

Things had not been the same since B.J.'s death. She still hated Annette for taking B.J.'s life the way that she did. That bitch had the nerve to come to the funeral and give a performance. Venus smiled remembering how Annette was thrown out by everyone after they found out who had pushed B.J. down the stairs, claiming it was an accident.

B.J. was eleven years younger than Venus and had won her heart. He was also the man who had broken her heart, cheating, and lying about it. He would still be alive if only he had not been cheating. Venus' thoughts made her bitter.

She remembered the food was on the stove and went back into the kitchen. She mixed the hamburger meat with the sauce and then drained the noodles. The aroma was overpowering. She checked her watch again, knowing that Andre would be coming in soon. His life was run by schedule and he was a creature of habit.

Venus hated and loved him at the same time. He could be so sweet and tender at times, and at other times he was a beast. She didn't want to start over so she stayed with him. Things between them got harder with every growing year. She often wondered if Andre knew he was bi-polar. Venus could always tell how the night would be by the mood he was in when he came in from work. If he had a bad day then he would take it out on her. If he had a good day then he would come in with wine, roses and or candy. They would make passionate love all night, and that is when she loved him the most.

He would hold her and they would cuddle up in front of the television. However, lately he was turning her love for him into hate. She prayed that he was having a good day but she would never know because she was forbidden to call him at work.

Andre was the bank manager at the same bank where they met. Venus had been promoted and was transferred to another location. She made a pitcher of fruit punch, added some ice. Then she put it in the refrigerator. She remembered how they met at the other bank. Andre was always trying to get Venus out to lunch. He would bring her lunch at her office. One day they made love on her desk. The thought made her laugh out loud.

"What's so funny?" a voice with a cold tone asked.

Distracted by the reminiscing, Venus had not heard Andre come in. Whenever he was in a bad mood he would creep in. Bullet and Diamond were out back and did not hear him. Normally they would bark and that would give her a heads up.

"Oh, nothing, baby," she answered, feeling guilty. "I was just thinking about when we did it on my desk. Do you remember the time?"

"Who cares," he replied, taking off his suit jacket and hanging it over the back of the chair.

"How was your day?" Venus asked, reaching out to give him a hug.

Andre sidestepped her, went into the kitchen, and took a beer out the refrigerator.

"Fix my plate," he ordered, before going into the bathroom to wash his hands.

Venus sat the pitcher of fruit punch on the table, went to the bathroom door, and asked Andre again, "Baby, how was your day?"

Andre turned to her with soap in his hands.

"Fix...my...plate," he slowly said in a firm voice.   Then he closed the door in her face.

"Bastard," Venus whispered.

She went to the kitchen and took out plates and utensils, and set the table. Andre came out the bathroom drying his hands.

"I hope there's garlic bread," he said.

"Uh, I didn't get a chance to make any. Do you want me to run out and get some rolls?" Venus asked, knowing the answer. Damn! How could she forget?

"You're a fuck up. How the hell are we supposed to have spaghetti without garlic bread?"

"I'm sorry," Venus said, putting her head down.

"I know you're sorry. A sorry ass," he said without emotion and sat at the table.

Without saying another word she sat down to eat. Andre twirled the noodles around the fork and put the hefty amount in his mouth. He chewed slowly. Venus watched the expression on his face and thought, what now. He twirled some more noodles and chewed even slower. Venus ate her food wondering what he could possibly have to complain about. She knew that she diced up everything, and the sauce was thick not watery. What was the problem? She mused.

Andre poured fruit punch into his glass, and in one gulp drank it all. He belched like a fat sailor before asking Venus, "What the hell do you think you're doing? Are you trying to kill me?"

Venus did not know what to say and decided to remain quiet. She saw that familiar madness in his eyes. Andre got up and closed the back door, locking the dogs out. She knew it was going to be a fight whenever he did that. The dogs would tear him up.

"Oh, you didn't hear me huh?" He got up and grabbed Venus by the hair. "Answer me!" he yelled like a mad man. "Are you fucking trying to kill me?" he reiterated while firmly yanking her head back and forth with every word.

"Ow! O-o-u-u-u-c-h! Andre you're hurting me!"

"I'm hurting you?" he asked incredulously. "You've got to be fucking kidding me!" he said, yanking harder. "You're trying to kill me, but I'm hurting you. Give me a fucking break!" He pushed her face into the plate and mushed it around. "Is it hot enough for you!" he yelled. "You eat it bitch! Eat!"

She had forgotten that she put black pepper in the sauce.

"Eat it since you like everything hot," he demanded, while pushing her face into the food.

"Stop it! Dammit!" she yelled.

Andre pulled Venus out of her chair. One hand was wrapped in her hair and the other around her throat. He dragged her into the bathroom while she kicked and clawed. Venus could not scream because he had her by the throat choking her. He threw her in the tub like she was dirty clothes that had missed the laundry.

"No-o-o-o!" she screamed trying to get out. "Andre, please no!" Andre turned on the hot water and held Venus down in the tub by stepping on her.

"Since you like everything hot then wash up!" He hollered.

Venus fought to get out of the tub, but Andre was stronger. She bit him on the leg while the hot water pelted her skin. He yelled out in pain and punched Venus in the face. Blood poured out of her nose while steam filled the bathroom.

"Andre, please stop," Venus begged as the water burned her.

He glanced at his leg bleeding through his pants.

"Shut up, cunt," he yelled, stomping out the bathroom.

Venus could hear the dogs barking like crazy, trying to get in. She crawled out of the tub, grabbed a towel and put it to her nose. She could hear Andre in the room ranting and raving. He was changing clothes, getting ready to fight for real. He was really pissed that she had bit him. Venus looked at herself in the mirror and decided to do the only thing she could do before Andre came out of the room. She ran barefooted and bloody out of the house.

CHAPTER SIX
NEW YORK

Share and Will were watching a movie when the phone rang. It was Venus calling collect. Will accepted the phone call, and stopped the movie before passing the phone to Share. This was not the first time. So he knew it was bad news when she called collect. Share took the telephone.

"Hello…"

Venus wasted no time talking quickly, telling her best friend what had happened. After listening Share said, "Get in a cab." Then she asked, "Are you hurt?"

"You'll see when I get there," Venus said before hanging up. Share hung up and told Will what had happened, as if he did not already know.

"Yeah, I figured that. She must like it, because she always stays with him."

"Will stop it," Share said, sighing. "She's just confused. You know she hasn't been right since… Well you know what happened to B.J."

"Yeah, well…" Will started to say something then his voice trailed.

It had been five years. The pain was still fresh. If it were not for B.J., Will would have never met Share. He had gotten Will the job at the McDonald franchise Share owned. Will had found a love that he thought he would never have because all he did was bone bitches and bounce. He thought about his man and how much he missed him. The way B.J. died at the hand of a skeezer because he cheated brought sorrow. Will never cheated on Share because he was happy with her. She made his heart smile. Share was ten years older than Will. Age difference was never an issue. Even when Share found out that she was HIV positive, Will told her that he wasn't going anywhere. He stood by her then and even more now. They used protection when making love so that he would not get infected. Their relationship was stronger than ever.

The horn beeping outside brought him out of his thoughts. It was a cab. Share stepped out of their brownstone on 142nd Street and paid the driver for the twelve-dollar trip. Venus got out of the cab looking like she had been through hell. Venus was at the door before Share had even gotten her change from the driver. She and Share hugged in the foyer with Venus breaking away.

"I don't want Will to see me like this."

She was embarrassed again, knowing Will would probably be judgmental and biased.

"Girl, he ain't thinking about you like that. You're family, and if anything Will's mad because you stay with that nutcase. Now come on," Share said.

Will was sitting in front of the television when they came in. He got up and hugged Venus tightly. She cried on his shoulder.

"It's alright sissy, we got you," Will assured Venus, rubbing her back. "When you're ready you know we'll take care of that nigga and he won't ever fuck wit' you again," Will said looking at her. She could feel the intensity in his gaze.

"Come on let's go get you cleaned up," Share said walking toward the bathroom.

Venus knew she was going to be alright. Share opened the medicine cabinet in her oversized bathroom and took out the alcohol and alcohol pads. Venus sat on the toilet seat and put her head in her hands. How many times would Share have to clean her up? Venus was tired of the situation, but didn't have the courage to leave Andre. Share cleaned the cut under Venus' nose.

"I want him out of my building. Tomorrow we'll go over there and get your clothes," Share said and left Venus in the bathroom.

"Okay," Venus said hoping it would be easy.

She knew Andre would not go without a fight. Venus turned on the shower and stripped. The water was a reminder of what Andre had just done to her. It didn't feel good, it was painful. Why did Andre do the things that he did to her? Why did he treat her like she was shit? Venus knew that she deserved better.

After the shower, Venus went to the back room and got on her knees. "There has got to be a better way…" she prayed.

Afterwards she pulled back the covers and went into the living room with Will and Share. Share looked back and asked, "How you feeling?"

"Better," Venus said, sitting down.

Venus felt like she was intruding knowing how much Share and Will valued their time together. She looked at them from the corner of her eye, and felt a rush of jealousy. She and B.J. would cuddle up to each other in front of a good movie.

"I'm going to bed now," Venus said, getting up slowly off the couch.

She hugged them both before going back to the guest room. Pulling back the covers, she got in the bed wincing at the pain that shot through her body. This was the result of Andre throwing her into the tub. She turned on her side, and her gut tightened up when the phone started ringing.

She could hear Share talking and getting angry. Then she heard the phone being slammed. It was comforting to have real friends. Venus smiled to herself. They always protected each other no matter what. It seemed like after what Share had been through with Petie, she had become stronger.

Moments later Share came in the room.

"That prick just called, and I told him not to call here anymore. He talking about 'let me speak to Venus', like he got it like that."

Venus laughed at the way Share imitated Andre. Share continued telling her that Will and his peeps were going to be on Andre's doorstep if he called back. "You already know how they do," Share said, cutting her eye at Venus.

Venus knew all too well. She remembered when Will and his team had put Petie in the hospital and damn near killed him for fucking with Share. Will played no games when it came to Share. If something upset her, then it upset him too. They were united as one.

"You get yourself some rest because we got a long day tomorrow," Share said, kissing her best friend's forehead.

"Good night, sista," Venus responded and turned over. She fell into restless sleep thinking about what tomorrow would be like.

CHAPTER SEVEN
BALTIMORE, MARYLAND

Petie pulled up in his driveway and parked behind the car driven by Patrice's mother, that was now in the driveway. She had come to care for Amir while they were at the doctor's office. He dialed Renee's telephone number anxious to hear what Darnell had done this time. Petie was ready to go out there and fuck Darnell up for stressing Renee. He was not going to allow Darnell to follow in his footsteps.

Renee answered on the third ring sounding breathless. Petie wasted no time asking her in detail what Darnell had done. Renee told him everything. Petie listened without saying a word until she was finished.

"Anything else?" he asked.

"No just all the other stuff you already know. I'm just tired of him, Petie. I don't know what more I can do," Renee said on the brink of tears.

"Put that nigga on the phone," Petie said in a no nonsense tone.

Renee called Darnell to the phone and waited for him to come down the steps. When he did, Renee loudly said, "Your father's on the phone. Now talk all that shit you were talking earlier so he can hear you, tough guy! Go head, gangsta!"

Petie heard Darnell say something that sounded muffled like he was trying to cover up the phone. Then Renee screamed, "Get on the phone, gangsta!"

Darnell's voice was weak when he said, "What's up dad?"

"You already know what the fuck is up, so why you asking

me, huh? Are you trying to be funny?" Petie asked his oldest son with coldness in his voice. Darnell did not answer; he was quiet as a mouse.

"I'm talking to you!" Petie yelled into the phone. "I asked you a fucken question that requires an answer."

"I don't know, dad," Darnell replied sounding like he was ten years old.

"You don't know? Well, I'll tell you what I'm gonna do... Your monthly allowance I'm gonna send that to Donte until you can figure out what's going on, since you don't know."

"But dad all," was all Darnell got to say before Petie cut him off.

"No, no. But dad what? You said that you didn't know. So I don't know what you could possibly do with your allowance, since you don't know anything. That means that you don't know how to spend it either, right? That means that you don't need it, right? So I figured that Donte would definitely know what to do with it, right? Don't you agree? I mean since you don't know anything."

"Dad, all I was saying was—"

Petie cut him off again and said, "It doesn't matter what you gonna say now because you had your chance to say everything when you first got on the phone, and you didn't. So anything you want to say now is bullshit. Now put your mother on the phone."

Renee got on the phone saying, "I'm here."

"Ahight, any more problems out of him and you call me immediately, ya heard?"

"Yes..."

"How you been doing besides that?" he asked.

"Alright, just working hard that's all."

"Are you good with money? Do you need anything?" he

asked with genuine concern.

"No, I'm good and thank you, baby."

"You know I love you and I always will. You heard?"

"Yes," she replied. Renee was smiling shyly but he would never know.

"Alright, call me in a couple of days," Petie said.

"Alright, good night…"

She hung up and sat back on the couch. Darnell went upstairs, stomping around. He still missed his father all these years, and that's why he was rebelling. Should she feel guilty about her and Petie's break up? Hell no, her inner voice told her. They had hit a bottom in their marriage and it was over. She and Petie were closer now than when they were living together as a family. He still took care of her sending her a thousand-dollars-a-month, plus he sent Darnell and Donte three-hundred dollars a piece each month. He was and had always been responsible when it came to his family. Nobody could ever take that away from Petie. He was a damn good father, but a lousy husband.

Feeling a little jealous, Renee wondered if he cheated on Patrice. She wondered if Patrice stayed awake at night wondering where he was like she used to do. Darnell and Donte went down south to see their father every other month for the weekend, for the pass three years since Petie bought his house. They seemed to like Patrice, telling Renee that she was good people. She always made them feel comfortable. Renee understood how Patrice felt. Patrice knew that no matter what Petie came home to her so she was very secure. She remembered when she had the same outlook. Secretly, she envied Patrice.

Petie went inside the house and helped Patrice get ready for her appointment. Patrice had just gotten dressed and was waiting for Petie in their sunken living room. She looked up at him when he walked in and smiled.

"I thought you were going to be late," she said, getting up off the Italian leather circular sofa.

"I could never be late for you, ma," Petie said, helping Patrice to her feet.

"Let's go, daddy. Maybe, we won't have to sit there all day," she said, walking out of the patio door to the driveway. "Mommy, we are leaving now," Patrice called out to her mother who was upstairs.

They arrived at the doctor's office a short while later. The place was crowded and Patrice took a seat while Petie registered her like always. She didn't know how but he was able to get her in ahead of everyone.

She saw a young girl with her son watching Petie it made Patrice smile. She was used to bitches watching her man. Petie was gorgeous with that gangsta lean. Petie looked even better with his dreads. It seemed like every woman alive had a thing for a man with dreads. She didn't mind because she was very secure in her relationship with Petie. She knew that he did his thing, but he never brought any bullshit home. Women never called his phone, popping shit and all that other drama men put women through. Her thoughts were interrupted when Petie sat down next to her.

"Do you want something to drink?" he asked rubbing her stomach.

"No baby, I'm good," she answered.

The nurse called for Patrice shortly after they arrived. Patrice went to the back with Petie and didn't see when he passed the receptionist fifty dollars, a favor for a favor. They went into the doctor's room where a technician was waiting for Patrice to do her ultrasound. The technician dictated everything that the baby was doing at that time. Petie started smiling when the technician told her that the baby was sucking her thumb and with the other hand she seemed to be rubbing her head. The baby weighed almost six pounds, was fully developed and all of her organs were working properly.

They left the office and went to Pathmark supermarket in the local shopping center. Petie parked the truck, got out, and opened Patrice's door. They went into the crowded supermarket and got two shopping carts and went to the produce aisle. Patrice loved her fruits and vegetables. She ate very healthy and got plenty of exercise. Patrice wanted to deliver a healthy baby without complications. Petie meanwhile was getting meats, cereals and juices. This was their system for cutting time down, food shopping. They met at the front of the store and got on the same line. Petie unloaded the two carts, and stood behind Patrice with his hand in his pocket on a knot of money, waiting to pay the food bill.

Outside a guy opened the door for them and offered to help them to the car.

"Yeah, grab those bags out of that cart," Petie said.

Something about the guy made him think. The guy was not a bum, he had no visible signs of crack abuse and his hands were not swollen like a dope-fiend's would be. Patrice opened the door, and the guy put over twenty bags of food in the back. He quickly helped Petie put the bags in the back and waited while Petie closed up the back. Petie helped Patrice in the truck and closed the door behind her. He walked around to the back of the truck and gave the guy twenty dollars.

"Thanks, I appreciate it, man. I never get no more than three dollars out here," he said.

Petie said nothing. He just studied the guy for a minute and then he asked, "What's your name?"

"Um… Tennessee," the guy replied after thinking about it for a minute.

This nigga had some kind of history that haunted him, because he had to pause for a few seconds before saying his name. Thinking he might be able to put him to work, Petie wanted to know more. The guy was in good shape, his clothes needed to be cleaned, but he didn't stink. Just then Patrice called out the window.

"Daddy let's go."

"I'm comin' ma," Petie answered then he turned to Tennessee and asked, "How long you gonna be out here?"

"Um, I don't really know. Why?"

Petie did not answer him. He didn't answer questions—he asked them.

"Try to be around tomorrow in the morning," he said and got in the truck.

"Alright, partner. I'll be here."

Partner, Petie thought. Where is this cat from…Idaho? He pulled out of the shopping center and headed home. He had something to do tonight and figured that a couple of hours of rest would do him good.

CHAPTER EIGHT
NEW YORK

Lydia slipped out of the restaurant after telling Ladelle that she had to run some errands. Instead of driving, she caught a cab on the corner, and took it downtown to the Doral Inn. At the hotel she went straight to the elevators, and took it to the fifth floor. She glanced down the hall, quickly checking room numbers. She found the room and knocked. Her lover opened the door immediately.

"What took you so long?" he asked closing the door behind her.

"I had to wait for the right time to get away. I have a lot of inventory being done and you're lucky I made it," she said, stepping out of her shoes.

"I'm lucky you made it? No, I think it would've been your loss not mine," her lover said, taking off his pants. He watched Lydia from the corner of his eye, and slowly unbuttoned his shirt.

"I don't have that much time," Lydia said anxiously.

"Me neither," he replied, pulling Lydia into him.

She got on her knees, wasting no time taking him into her mouth, and raising him for the occasion. He returned the deed and got her moist and wet before turning her over on her knees. Her lover entered her slowly, and then picked up the pace while he stroked her with hunger. He pulled Lydia's hair, and arched her back to his liking while he slid in and out of her. She was tight and it made him want her more. Lydia moaned quietly enjoying the stroking that she was deprived of at home.

They climaxed at the same time. Their bodies shook until they separated. Lydia was the first to go to the bathroom and turned on the shower. She came out and took her brush out of her pocketbook and combed her hair back before getting in the shower. She scrubbed between her legs and the insides of her thighs with a generous amount of the hotel soap. Luckily, Ladelle was not the type of man to smell her when she was away from him. Lydia thought she always smelled like sex. The guilt of knowing that she was cheating on her man made her cleansing even more intense. Her lover was already dressed when she came out of the bathroom. Lydia gave him a look over and then said, "No shower for you, huh?"

He adjusted his tie and replied, "No, I want to keep your scent on me for the remainder of the day. I can work better like that."

He smiled slyly at her as she dried. Lydia gave him a quick kiss and hurriedly got dressed. He was at the door by the time she was finished.

"I'll see you in a couple of days," he said and left the room before she could respond.

Lydia waited; giving him enough time to exit the hotel before she left. Downstairs, she hailed a cab and headed back to the restaurant. She never saw a man across the street, snapping away digital pictures of her exiting the hotel and hopping into a cab.

CHAPTER NINE
PENNSYLVANIA

Every morning, Renee was the first person to leave the house. Darnell did nothing all day, and Donte was weeks away from graduating high school.

"Donte, make sure you get out on time!" Renee shouted on her way out the door.

"I will, mom," Donte called back.

She closed the door and got in her car. Tonight she and Cliff were going to spend some intimate time with each other. Renee was looking forward to it. She pulled out her driveway and turned on Chester Pike, heading to work. She was anxious for the day to be over. Donte got out of the shower and hurriedly dressed so that he wouldn't be late. Darnell was in the kitchen eating cereal when Donte came downstairs. He asked Donte, "So what you doin' after school?"

"Going to pick up Sonya and go to her house. Why?" Donte asked pouring cereal into a bowl.

"Just askin'," Darnell said eating his AppleJacks.

Donte wanted to talk to Darnell about yesterday and the way he disrespected their mother, but he knew it would only lead to a fight. He just hoped that Darnell and his mother worked it out. Darnell took his bowl into the living room, and ate his cereal in silence. He had plans for today that caused him to smile.

Renee drove down Chester Pike, listening to a Mary-Mary CD as she drove to work. She had been extra careful after a string of car jackings had left the small-populated community in fear. It seemed as if it would start to rain soon and the light morning traffic was slowing.

Renee hated to drive in the rain ever since witnessing an accident that left the female driver pinned under her car. Something about the rain made her think that it was an accident waiting to happen. She slowed down to thirty-five miles per hour as the rain came down heavier. Renee decided to pull over and wait for the rain to stop. She pulled into the 7-Eleven, across from the trolley station and sat there thinking, she'd be late for work but she'd rather be late than dead. People on the move came in and out of the busy store with cups of coffee and newspapers under their arms as they made their way back to their cars or to catch the trolley.

Renee turned off her engine and got out. She noticed a man with a hoodie over his head. He appeared to be out of place in the rush hour crowd. She walked inside the convenience store, looking back at him. He had his back turned, and acted as if he was looking for someone. Renee got on line, all the while wondering what this guy could be up to. I'm from Harlem, I'll fuck him up. Her mind was in overdrive, keeping a watchful eye as she made her coffee. Renee paid for her coffee, a cinnamon roll and the morning paper. She secured her change in her pocketbook, and headed back to her car.

The rain was pelting heavier now. Renee got behind the wheel and called her job to let them know that she was going to be late. She was the receptionist at a mental health clinic in Sharon Hill, and Renee had only missed three days in two years. She could barely see out of the windshield because of the heavy rain. She heard what she thought was a woman screaming. Then she saw a car reversing at top speed. The woman was soaking wet, pointing and screaming.

"He stole my car! My God somebody help me!"

Renee almost dropped her coffee at the excitement. The woman frantically ran in and out of the store screaming. People came out of the store and looked at the woman, wondering was this some kind of joke. Renee could see the guy speeding out of the parking lot on the slippery streets. She backed her car up and pulled out of the seven eleven just as quick as he did. She didn't know what she was doing—she was just doing it.

The car was speeding down Chester Pike and almost hit a turning car. Renee got on her cellphone and dialed 911, while trying to keep up with the speeding maniac. Through her headset she told the operator that she was following someone who had just stolen the car from the seven eleven.

"Ma'am you say that you are following the car now?" the operator asked calmly.

"Yes, he's speeding down Chester Pike. I don't know how long I can keep up with him. We're headed toward Darby. You better get some cops out here because I can't keep up with him too much longer. He's driving like a maniac. He just ran a red light," Renee said keeping the 911 operator informed.

"Okay ma'am you're doing well. The police have been dispatched. You should see them right about now. Please stay on the line."

"I see them! They turned in front of me," Renee excitedly said.

It was like she was doing some kind of undercover work. The police sirens screamed and chased the maniac driver through wet, dangerous traffic. Renee stayed a safe distance behind. The maniac was being chased by three police cars. He wasn't getting away. Cars pulled over to the side of the road as the car chase became more dangerous on the slippery wet busy streets.

Renee was caught at the light and she strained her eyes to keep up with the melee as rain pelted her windshield. The light changed and she took off like she was a cop, curious to see how this ended. They were heading toward Main Street when the maniac driver made a wild turn. The tires couldn't hold out and the car flipped over and slid into the busy bus terminal on its hood.

Pedestrians screamed, jumped out of the way and took cover. The police jumped out of their vehicles with guns drawn, and ordered the driver out of the overturned car. Renee got out of her car and watched from across the street. The car jacking, maniac driver was pulled out of the vehicle, and thrown on the ground.

Renee ran over to one of the officers to tell them that she had witnessed the entire incident and called 911.

"Okay, ma'am you did a fine job. Stand over here so we can get some information from you," the officer said wiping rain off of his glasses.

"Okay," Renee said feeling really good.

She was wondering if she'd be in the newspapers for her heroic deed as police handcuffed the driver and pulled him to his feet. They took him to a waiting car. Renee looked on in disbelief. Her eyes popped opened, blinking in rapid succession. She couldn't believe who she was seeing. The hoodie had fallen off the maniac driver's head and he was pushed into the squad car.

"My God," she whispered.

The carjacker was Calvin. He was Cliff's son.

CHAPTER TEN
NEW YORK

Share and Venus decided that it would be best to wait until Andre left for work before going over there. Venus called the bank to let them know that she would be late due to family emergency. The bank was more concerned with her situation and gave her time off.

Share and Venus arrived at Share's brownstone. This was the place Venus had hoped to turn into a place of love for her and Andre. Venus went to the back door and let the dogs in so that she could feed them. Andre had left them out there all night. She knew they were hungry. Share sat on the couch and shook her head. Looking around she said, "If he thinks he's going to be staying here, well he's got another thing coming."

"Oh, he'll be out of here, one way or the other," Venus agreed, filling the dogs' bowls up with water.

She went into the bedroom and removed clothes from the closet. Venus packed her Coach Carry with enough outfits for the rest of the week. In a smaller Coach case, she loaded up her cosmetics and bottles of perfume. Share walked to the back and looked out making a mental note to have the handyman come and whack the weeds in the backyard.

"Venus, what time does Andre get home from work?" Share asked.

"Around six—six-thirty… I'm sure he'll be calling when he comes in and I'm not here," Venus said, carrying her bags into the living room area.

Venus left extra food in the dogs' bowls before rolling the luggage to the door.

"Do you have everything you need?" Share asked picking up one of the bags.

"Yeah, let's go. I gotta get to work before ten," Venus said, picking up her keys off the table.

They went to the car and put the luggage in the backseat. Both of them were silent for the ride back to Share's house. Share double parked and helped Venus put the luggage into the foyer.

"I gotta go sista. I have a board meeting to attend, and I don't want to be late," Share said, reaching out.

"Okay, I'll see you when I get in," Venus said, hugging her best friend.

Share got in her car and drive off. Venus took a deep breath and rolled the luggage into the guest room. She quickly showered and dressed in gray slacks, matching silk blouse, and suede pumps. She slipped on a red blazer, pinned her hair into a bun, and called a cab.

Forty-five minutes later, she arrived at work, and headed straight to her office. Once she got situated, Venus checked her voice mail. She was not surprised to have two messages from Andre. The sound of his voice made her sick to her stomach. A frown appeared as she listened. Venus deleted both messages and settled in behind her desk. Her work day was going to be a good one despite what was going on. She never took her home life to work. She was busy working until Andre called.

"Andre, we've been through this before. I'm tired of the same old thing. You have to get yourself some help in order for this relationship to work," Venus paused listening to him breathe on the other end of the phone. She knew he was thinking of something to say.

Finally he said, "Okay, just come home so we can talk...

Please. I'll order something for us to eat and we'll have a nice, quiet evening and talk about it."

"I'll call you later. I really can't talk about it right it now," Venus hung up the phone before he could respond.

She wanted to tell him to pack his stuff and leave but could not muster the courage. She knew that Share would handle his eviction and that made her smile.

Later that afternoon Venus called Share and told her that she was going home.

"Talk to him about what?" Share exclaimed. "There's nothing to talk about! I don't think that you should go."

"I'm not staying, I'm just going to talk and let him know that he has to move. He's talking about having dinner."

"Me and Will are gonna meet you there."

"No, I'll be alright, sista. I'll call you when I get there."

"I love you and you know I only want the best for you. You call us if he blinks too hard," Share said.

"I will, sista," Venus said, laughing.

She hung up the phone, double checked her assigned accounts, before logging out of her terminal. Venus decided to leave early so she could get home before Andre did. She was hoping that tonight would not end up in a fight, but if it did then he would be leaving in handcuffs. She was not going to spare him his reputation in the banking world anymore.

Venus got out of the cab, and walked to the corner store to get dog food. She remembered that the food was running low and Andre wouldn't bother to get dog food.

Bullet and Diamond greeted her inside the first floor apartment. They growled and barked until they saw who it was. They jumped all over her. Venus took out a couple of minutes and rubbed the pit bulls on their stomachs before taking the bag into the kitchen. Venus thought about leaving before Andre came home and just leaving a note for him telling him to leave, but she wanted to hear what he had to say. She took off her shoes, and put her briefcase down. Then she made herself a quick drink. If Andre had a fight on his mind today, well she was going to fight his ass back.

Venus turned on the television and sat down to watch CNN. She called Share to tell her that she was home and was waiting for Andre to come in.

"Don't let that bastard sweet talk you, sista. Say what you got to say and make sure that he knows that I want his ass out of my building," Share said sounding all business.

She never really liked Andre from the beginning and only dealt with him on the strength of her best friend. She always told Venus that something wasn't right about him.

"Oh, I'm not falling for any of his bullshit tonight. Believe me Share, I'll be fine," Venus said.

They talked until Andre came in with Venus saying, "I hear his key in the door now, plus the dogs just ran to the front. I'll call you when I'm leaving".

"Alright," Share said.

Seconds later, Andre walked in, a box of chocolate in one hand and his briefcase in the other. He smiled perfectly when he saw Venus. She didn't smile back but turned the channel on the television and totally ignored him. Andre moved smoothly over to where Venus was sitting on the couch and kissed her gently on the lips. She turned her head slightly. His touch made her sick. Just twenty-four hours ago he was holding her down under scalding hot water and pushing her face in spaghetti and now today he wanted to be nice.

Beat it, rabbit, she thought. She was ready to say what she had to say and leave.

"How was your day?" he asked, putting down his briefcase and locking the door.

"Fine," Venus said.

She reached for the remote control and turned the television off. Venus turned, facing Andre.

"I'm leaving you for good this time," she said. "You've got seventy-two hours to get out of Share's building, or she will be taking legal action against you."

Andre stood stock-still listening to Venus. He glared at her like she was the enemy. After an awkward, long silence, Venus asked, "Did you hear what I said?"

"Yeah, I heard you. Obviously you've thought long and hard about this so there's no point in me trying to change your mind," he stated and walked to the kitchen.

"Well, then I guess there's nothing else to discuss," Venus said, getting off the couch.

She walked pass him and went into the bedroom to get some more clothes. She put some shoes in a bag and was getting some lingerie when she heard the back door open and close. Andre was letting the dogs out. She knew what was coming.

Venus walked out of the bedroom and into the kitchen. Andre was leaning against the counter, smirking and shaking his head. Another second, he was in her face yelling and screaming like a mad man. He head butted Venus knocking her to the floor. She was dazed by the blow. Her vision was blurry and she tried hard to refocus. He stood over her, rolling up his sleeves. This was her opening. She kicked him in the groin.

Andre doubled over, wincing in pain. She scrambled to get to her feet and he tripped her knocking her back down. Andre jumped on her back, punching her in the kidneys. Venus screamed in pain, trying to turn over on her side. The dogs were barking and scratching to get inside but couldn't. Venus managed to turn over, raking her nails down Andre's face. He screamed and grabbed at his bleeding face.

Venus got quickly to her feet, yelling for help. She got her hand on the top lock. Andre grabbed a handful of her hair and threw her back like a rag doll. The back of Venus' head hit the edge of the table and she bounced to the floor. Andre stood over her motionless body and kicked her. "Get up, bitch," he yelled. "You wanted to fight so let's fight!"

Venus didn't move. He kicked her again, only to find her not moving at all. The dogs barked ferociously at the back door clawing and chewing at the screen to get in. Andre bent down and nudged Venus with his hand. There was no response.

"Get up!" he yelled, panicking. He looked back and screamed at the door, "Shut up!"

The dogs barked and growled louder at him. Andre started pacing back and forth. He felt Venus' neck for a pulse and it was light. He grabbed his head in frustration and started punching on the floor. "Wake up, dammit!" he begged. He tried to pull Venus to her feet but her body was not responding. Andre grabbed the phone and dialed 911. He told the operator that Venus had fallen and bumped her head and was not moving.

"Okay sir, I'm dispatching EMS now," the operator said.

Andre waited for further instructions and shortly afterwards he could hear the sirens blaring from a distance. He ran into the bathroom and tried to cover up the scratch marks on his face but they could not be hidden. Venus would have the last word. The scratch marks on his face spoke volumes.

CHAPTER ELEVEN
PENNSYLVANIA

Darnell closed the door behind him, and ran outside to his friend Rodney, waiting for him. Darnell got in the passenger's seat and gave his friend a pound. "What's good?" Rodney asked.

"Nothin' much I'm ready to get out of here and go down south with my dad. This lady is mad corny," Darnell said, referring to Renee.

He leaned back in his seat as his friend pulled away from the curb. Darnell reached into his pocket and pulled out a rolled blunt and lit it with his lighter.

"So where we headed?" Rodney asked.

He was infatuated with Darnell being from New York. Darnell was like a God to him. Rodney had never been out of Pennsylvania and Darnell was like a real 'G' to him.

"I want to go by the high school and pick somebody up," Darnell said taking a long pull on his blunt. He blew out the smoke slowly and then said, "I want to catch up with this chick before she leaves".

"Anybody I know?" Rodney asked, reaching for the blunt. Darnell didn't answer.

They stopped for a red light, and Rodney puffed quickly then passed it before the light changed. They drove to Chester and stopped at the high school on Ninth Street. Darnell got out of the car and leaned on the side checking out the girls walking in-groups. A lot of the girls knew Darnell from his reputation and the fact that he was from New York. They all spoke and gave him seductive looks as they walked pass. Darnell had fucked most of them and then moved on to their friends. He wasn't interested in any of them. He had his mind on Sonya. She was Donte's girl.

Darnell wanted to test her loyalty. Was the bitch faithful or was she another one of them birds that should be in the sky? He waited patiently until she came out of the front exit. She wasn't expecting Darnell to be there so when she saw him, she was surprised.

"What's up Darnell?" she asked smiling naively.

"How are you doing?" Darnell asked smiling.

He got off the car, and removed Sonya's backpack from her shoulder.

"What's up? Is Donte around?" she asked, looking into the car.

"Nah, he asked me to pick you up and bring you to the crib after you dropped off your books at home," Darnell lied.

Sonya thought about it for a moment and said, "Oh…okay".

She got in the backseat, greeted Rodney, and fastened her seatbelt. "You know where I live right, Darnell?"

"Yeah, in the Fairgrounds," he replied, getting back into the car.

Rodney pulled into traffic and drove to Sonya's house and parked in front of her building. Darnell was out of the car first and he told Rodney, "I'll be right out. Turn the car off."

"Alright," Rodney said.

Darnell and Sonya walked to her building. She took out her key and opened the front door. Darnell walked in behind her and set the backpack on the floor. He stood by the door and looked around before speaking.

"Is your mother home?" he asked.

"No, she's at work," Sonya said.

She went into the kitchen and came out eating an apple. She

asked Darnell if he wanted anything.

"No, I'm good."

"Okay, well have a seat. I gotta go change and I'll be right out," Sonya said, going into her room.

Darnell waited until she closed her door then he locked the front door. He closed the blinds, walked to Sonya's room, and stood outside her door for a few seconds. Darnell waited until he heard the jingle from her belt hit the floor and then he turned the knob and opened her door. Sonya turned around quickly and said, "What the fuck are you doing, Darnell?"

"Just trying to get what my little brother gets," he said, unfastening his belt.

Sonya yelled, "Get the fuck out of my room you bastard!"

Darnell pushed her on the bed and tore at her blouse. She screamed. He covered her mouth, and held her down while he pulled his manhood out. She scratched and clawed at him and he punched her in the jaw. Sonya screamed out in pain and kicked Darnell in his jewels. He tumbled off of the bed and rolled on the floor. She ran half-naked out of the apartment and over to her neighbor's house.

Darnell got to his knees and pulled up his zipper and went out through her bedroom window on the side of the building. He limped back to Rodney's car.

"Drive," he ordered.

Rodney started the car asking was everything all right? Darnell lied and said that Sonya was too aggressive and he had to run out of there.

"Oh, are you serious?" Rodney blurted, impressed by what Darnell said.

"Yeah, she's bugged out. She wants it too much," Darnell continued.

He sat back in his seat knowing that all hell was going to break loose. He told Rodney to go down by the water so they could smoke their blunt and then he wanted to go home because he had something to do.

"All right, my dude," Rodney uttered.

They drove down to the pier and smoked the remainder of the blunt with Darnell in deep thought getting his story ready.

Renee was about to go out for lunch when Sonya's mother called her on her cellphone.

"Hi Renee this is Nicole, Sonya's mother."

"Hey, how you doing…?" Renee asked.

"Not so good. Um Darnell… Well I don't know how to say this, so I'm just gong to get right to the point. Darnell attacked Sonya a little while ago…"

Renee almost dropped her cellphone. "He did what?"

"Yeah, he uh, picked her up from school and offered a ride home and then when they got there…well he tried to rape her," Nicole explained slowly.

Renee could hear the anger in her voice and she could tell that Nicole was trying to be calm. Renee did not know what to say, but she believed Nicole, knowing that Sonya would not make up anything like that. Sonya was a good girl, and Renee loved her from the first time Donte brought her home. Renee was disgusted knowing that Darnell would do something so horrible. It reminded her when Petie had raped Share and then fled down south.

"Nicole, I am so sorry. Is Sonya okay?" Renee inquired with genuine sincerity.

"Yeah, she's just shook up. She can't believe he did something like that to her... I just wanted to call you before I call the police and report it."

"Yes I understand, Nicole. I'm leaving work now and going home so I can see if he's there because I know he won't answer the phone. Um Nicole, I know this is difficult for you and I don't want to offend you by asking you this, but is there anyway we can leave the police out of this?"

"Absolutely, not," Nicole responded quickly.

"I'm only asking because I was sending Darnell to his father this week anyway, and now in light of this, I want him out of my house today," Renee said, hoping that she would agree.

Nicole said nothing for a few seconds that seemed to take forever and then she spoke.

"Renee, this is very troubling for me. And I'll take your word that Darnell will be out of this state by the end of the week. The last thing I want to do is have you dragged through the mud because of him. So yes, I'll work with you on this," Nicole agreed clearly against what she wanted to do.

She knew that Renee was under all a lot of pressure already from Darnell and she agreed.

"Oh, I can assure you that his ass will be out of here within the next forty-eight hours. I want to get home so I'll call you later and check on Sonya," Renee said before hanging up.

She clicked off her cellphone and went to the bathroom. Renee checked to make sure that no one else was in there before banging on the stall door. She was so furious that tears were streaming down her face. Renee put cold water on her face and tried to calm herself down. She couldn't believe Darnell would do something so horrible. Renee pulled herself together and went back to her desk. She called her supervisor to tell her that she had to leave early because she had an emergency. Her supervisor asked, "Will you be in tomorrow?"

"Yes, I just have an emergency with my oldest son," Renee stated without going into details.

Her co-workers were looking at her like she was a hero for following the carjacker this morning. Renee didn't feel like a hero after seeing that the driver was Calvin, her male friend's son. Now this bullshit with Darnell was the icing on the cake. Renee snatched her pocketbook out of her desk drawer and walked briskly to the parking lot. She jumped in behind the wheel, anxious to get home. She was hoping that Darnell wasn't there because she could see herself killing him.

Renee arrived at her house in record time. She sat behind the wheel and prayed that her problematic son was not home. Needing time to calm down, she inhaled deeply. When she opened the front door, she called out to him. No answer. Anger overcame Renee, she ran up the stairs ready to punch Darnell in his face. Renee pushed his bedroom door open but there was no sign of him. She looked out the back window to see if he was sitting out in the backyard like he sometimes did. She went back downstairs to get her cellphone from her pocketbook. She called Darnell on his cellphone not expecting him to answer when he would see her number. His phone rang until the voicemail picked up. Renee hung up and redialed. The phone rang four times and the voicemail answered. He had to be looking at her number and ignoring it.

She called Petie to tell him what had happened. Patrice answered the phone on the second ring and told Renee that Petie was out back and she would have him call her back.

"Okay, please tell him to hurry. It's an emergency," Renee told her.

"Okay, I will. I'll make sure he calls you right back," Patrice responded.

Renee hung up and went upstairs to the bathroom. She took her medicine out of the cabinet and shook a pill out of each bottle. She carried them downstairs to the kitchen and took three. The phone rang before she could take the last three pills. Renee reached for the phone by the refrigerator.

"Hello…"

"What happened?" Petie asked her.

"I'll tell you what happened…" Renee said.

CHAPTER TWELVE
NEW YORK

Share was on her way to meet Will for dinner when she got the call about Venus. Share pulled over to the curb and stopped driving so she could hear exactly what had happened.

"Is she alright?" she asked the officer who was calling.

Share was Venus' emergency contact if anything ever happened to her and the 40th Precinct was well aware of the problems in Venus' relationship. They had been called to Venus' house several times but Venus never pressed charges on Andre.

"Yeah, well we don't know yet. She's been taken to Lincoln Hospital. She's being treated for head trauma. The boyfriend called it in and said that she had fell. When we arrived she was unconscious and unresponsive," the officer informed Share.

"I'm going to the hospital now. I'll be there as soon as I can," Share told him.

She closed her cellphone and sped into traffic, running a red light then making an illegal U-turn. Dammit! Share's thoughts raced while tears streamed down her face. She had told Venus not to go because Andre could not be trusted. She called Will who was at the Olive Garden waiting for her. She told him to meet her at the hospital. Share arrived at the hospital in record time considering traffic. She double-parked and jumped out of her car rushing into the hospital. At the nurses' station she identified herself and asked if she could see Venus. Share was told to talk to the doctor who was treating Venus.

"Where is he?"

"I'll page him for you ma'am. Just have a seat and wait," the nurse said.

She picked up the phone, paged the doctor then turned to Share and said, "Now we just have to wait until he calls back. He's normally pretty quick."

Share was so mad, she didn't even want to sit, so she paced. She ran outside looking for a police officer, maybe one who had responded to the 911 call. She approached four officers standing by their vehicles and asked if any of them were the escorting officers from 408 East 144th Street.

"No, ma'am that would be Myers and Wilson, they're over there to your left," one of the officers said pointing.

"Thank you very much," Share said and went to speak to them.

She introduced herself, shaking hands and then asking them were they treating this as a domestic violence case. The two officers exchanged looks before the senior one replied, "Well, at this time we are looking into the prospect that this is a D.V. The boyfriend is being questioned at the station now."

"Yeah, well you make sure you charge that asshole, because this was no accident. He tried to kill her. He's been beating on her for as long as they've been together. The police at 40th are well aware of the violence in the relationship."

"Okay ma'am, can you come down to the precinct and talk to the detectives?"

"Of course I will. That's my best friend and I'll do whatever it takes to make sure that he gets charged," Share said with a serious stone face.

She told the officers that she wanted to go and talk to the doctor before she went to the precinct. Share went back inside the hospital and spotted Will sitting in the waiting area. She walked quickly to him and he got up and hugged her. Share cried softly on his shoulder while he whispered, "She'll be alright. Don't worry, ma she'll be alright."

The doctor approached with a nurse to talk to Share. She wiped her eyes and faced him while he explained that Venus had a concussion and swelling of her frontal lobe. There was intensive swelling, and blood clot they fear could be aneurysm. The doctors were treating her with I.V. blood thinners and intravenous nourishment.

"My god is she going to be okay?"

"Only time will tell. She's getting the best of care."

"When can I see her?"

"I'll take you to see her now for a moment," the doctor said, guiding Share to the ICU. She saw Venus lying still in the hospital bed, and tears like waterfall came running down her face. That bastard was going to pay for this, she thought holding her best friend's hand gently. She and Will stayed for as long as they were allowed. Share quietly prayed while Will stared with anger all over his face. Thirty minutes later, the doctor escorted them out, and they left heading for the precinct.

Share walked into the precinct like she owned it. She was quickly referred to the detective handling Venus' case.

"Detective Reynolds will be right down," the desk sergeant said, making a call.

Moments later, a tall, slim, clean shaven, man, wearing jeans, and tie that didn't match, greeted them. After introducing himself, he led them upstairs to an overcrowded room with desks side by side. He sat down and opened a file before asking Share what kind of information she had. Share told him about all the fights that Venus and Andre had over the years, ending with the most recent one.

"So you're saying that last night they were fighting?" Detective Reynolds asked, writing in his note pad.

"Yes, she had to run out of the house barefooted and catch a cab. She was crying and bloodied when she came to my house. I had told her earlier today not to go home. Unfortunately, she thought that she'd be okay so she did anyway. This man lives in the building that I own. I had told Venus that I was putting him out. She wanted to get some more clothes to last her until he left," Share explained.

"What exactly is your relationship to her?"

"She's my best friend."

"Where is he at now?" Will inquired.

"We're holding him in a cell. You see when we arrived on the scene, he was acting very nervous and on edge. He wasn't acting like someone who was afraid for his girlfriend. He seemed to my partner and me that he was more afraid of us. The first thing we noticed was that he had some scratch wounds to his face and neck that was a sign of something domestic going on, so we held him," Detective Reynolds explained.

He had a no nonsense look about him that Share liked immediately.

"I just left the hospital. She has a concussion and swelling on her brain. She didn't even know that we were there. She's not responding to anything right now. The doctor said that she has a blood clot forming that they fear might be an aneurysm but they have to run more tests. Please, don't let him get away with this, detective. This man is violent don't let him walk on this," Share pleaded.

"Oh, he won't walk on this. I can assure you. I have seen many domestic violence cases, and this one had D.V. written all over it. As of now he's being charged with first degree assault, and anything else I can think of before he goes in front of the judge. I'd like to make a stop by the hospital and check on the victim's condition. I'll get a better insight on exactly what we'll charge him with," Detective

Reynolds said directly to Share.

Share was satisfied with what she had heard, and reached out her hand saying, "I'd like to thank you for your time, Detective Reynolds. Please keep in contact if you need me for anything." She handed him her business card before she and Will left the precinct.

In his holding cell, Andre sat on the cold, steel slab bench, and held his head in his hands. He could not believe that he was being detained. Did they know who he was? Did these dicks have any idea that he could cause them a lot of problems? He had already been in there for nearly three hours and these assholes weren't telling him shit. Was he being charged or what? He thought bitterly. He couldn't take the waiting game anymore. Andre got up, went to the bars, and started calling for an officer.

"Hello! Hello! Is anybody there?"

Moments later an officer came by and asked, "Whaddaya want?"

"I want to go home that's what I want," Andre replied sarcastically.

"Yeah, well you gotta wait for your arresting officer to come down," the officer said and walked away.

"How long is that gonna be? I gotta go to work in the morning."

Before the officer could answer Detective Reynolds came down to the holding cells and told the officer, "I'll take it from here."

He shot a cold stare at Andre with and said, "Look pal, as of now you're being charged with assault and battery in the first degree. As soon as I'm done with the paperwork, I'll get transportation to take you downtown. Relax, because it's going to be a while."

"Are you out of your mind?" Andre exclaimed while grabbing on the bars. "I don't have time for this bullshit! I run a bank you asshole! You're going to regret this! I want to call my goddamn lawyer, now!"

Detective Reynolds looked at Andre, unimpressed by his insults.

"You'll get your phone call, pal. Just relax," the experienced detective said.

"I'm not your pal, asshole! I want to speak to my lawyer!" Andre yelled like a little kid who wanted to come out of their room.

The commotion in the holding cell attracted the attention of a few officers. They came down to see what was going on. Detective Reynolds smiled at them as they huddled around him asking was he all right.

"Yeah, I'm fine. This asshole thinks he can damn near kill his girl and walk out of here. I was just telling him that it doesn't work that way," he told them.

"Oh, we got a wife beater, huh?" one of the plain clothes officers asked.

He was a big, brawly redneck that looked like he had been in plenty of barroom brawls. He pointed his finger at Andre and shouted, "You shut the fuck up down here, asshole! I don't want to hear all this noise on my goddamn tour! If I gotta come in there to shut you up, it's not gonna be pretty, my friend. Do you hear me, asshole?"

Andre mumbled inaudibly and moved away form the bars. He sat down on the steel bench. This was a no win situation. He remained quiet as the bad boys loudly joked outside the cell. Andre heard but didn't respond. He decided to wait patiently until they gave him his phone call. His mind started wondering to a time when he was younger and his life was just beginning. His first girlfriend that he thought he would have a future with, kissing her for first time, the first time he slapped her. The first time he killed someone. Yeah, nobody had ever suspected anything until Jamie.

CHAPTER THIRTEEN
BALTIMORE, MARYLAND

Petie was reeling from what Renee had told him. He was ready to throw the phone at the wall. He had told Renee to put Darnell on the next train out of PA to Baltimore.

"I will, but he's not answering his phone. He knows I'm calling him and he isn't answering. The girl's mother was ready to call the police, and thank God I was able to talk her out of doing so. I just don't know what the fuck is wrong with him," Renee said.

"I have his number. You get him on a train out of there tonight. When I reach him, I'll tell him to go home and start packing," Petie told Renee.

"I'm going to pack his stuff now. Tell him to come home without the attitude," Renee said.

She was ready to pack her oldest son off to live with Petie. There was no other way. That was where Darnell wanted to be. If it was going to save his life then let him go, Renee thought.

Petie called Darnell's phone and Darnell answered on the second ring.

"Hey, dad," Darnell said.

"Yo, what the fuck is wrong with you? Are smoking crack or something?" Petie barked into the phone.

"No, dad," Darnell answered sounding like a little boy.

"We're gonna have a nice long fucken talk when you get here. Your mother is packing your shit right now. You get your ass home and don't give her any problems. You know that lady is ready to call the police on you? Is that what you want?"

"No dad, I just want to come out there wit' you. Mommy's a hater. She been trying to keep me away from you for years and I don't want to be out here anymore," Darnell said.

Petie knew that Darnell came down south every month so how was Renee trying to keep them apart. He exploded on Darnell.

"That ain't any fucken excuse! Listen, you just get home and get your stuff. Whatever you can't carry you can go back for it later. Ya heard me?"

"Yeah dad, I'm going now," Darnell said, sounding a little bit more upbeat.

"Yo, Darnell if your mother calls me and tells me that you came in the crib acting up, I promise you I will break your fucken jaw. You heard?" Petie said.

"Dad, I'm not going to say anything to her. That's my word on everything I love," Darnell said.

Petie hung up without saying anything else. There was nothing else left to say. Petie changed clothes and put on a sweat suit before heading out. He had to go meet up with Chaos. They had some people coming in from Virginia to cop some work and Petie had to get into business mode. He would deal with Darnell when his wayward son arrived.

Patrice was in the kitchen cooking salmon cakes, brown rice and sweet peas. He leaned into her and kissed the back and the sides of her neck.

"Who loves you?" he asked.

She smiled from ear to ear and then replied, "You do."

Petie turned Patrice around and kissed her seductively before saying, "Don't ever forget that you heard?"

"I won't, daddy."

Amir sat at the table, watching the passionate exchange between his parents. Petie walked over to him, lifted his youngest son out of the chair, and gave him a kiss. Amir beamed saying, "Daddy, can I go with you?"

"Nah baby boy, daddy's got work to do. Tomorrow is your day, okay?"

"Okay, daddy," Amir was animated in his agreement.

Petie turned to Patrice and told her that Darnell was coming out to stay with them for a while. Patrice continued seasoning the rice and then said, "Okay, I'll get the spare room ready for him. I think there are clean sheets in the linen closet that he can use."

Petie looked at her admiringly, she was such an understanding woman, he thought. Patrice never asked any questions or put up a fight. She just went with the flow like a real woman should. Petie got in the truck and drove to his spot where he had to meet Chaos and Country. They were waiting for him when he pulled up in the back of the house. The dogs were chained around the backyard with heavy-duty chains. Petie went into the living room and met with Chaos.

"Did he call?" he asked Chaos who was sitting in front of a briefcase stacked with kilos.

"Yeah, they should be here in about another two hours," Chaos said, closing the briefcase.

Country entered the room and sat down on the couch across from Petie. He was Petie's original partner when Petie had first arrived. Things had changed since they first met. Country was not trustworthy anymore. Money had come up missing, he had made a few small deals behind Petie's back and one of Petie's contacts had said that he had seen Country using on several occasions. That was definitely a no-no.

Petie was just waiting for the right time to get rid of him. He couldn't just let Country go. He would have to kill him because he knew too much. Country had to be made ghost. To Chaos he said, "Let's take a ride."

Chaos got up and put the briefcase in the closet. Petie gave him a signal in the look they shared. They left out together. When they got in the truck, Petie told Chaos that he wanted to check on the guy from Pathmark, figuring Tennessee would be out there.

"What guy...the one that be begging for change?" Chaos asked with his nose turned up.

"Yeah, that's him. I'm trying to figure this cat out," Petie said and turned the corner. "He helped with the bags and I was checking him out. The nigga isn't a crack head that's for sure. He just needs a little help or something," Petie said, pulling into the shopping mart parking lot.

"Help... nigga we ain't Red Cross. Let the nigga get some help from somebody else," Chaos voiced his opinion with a screw face.

Petie ignored him while he parked the truck and scanned the parking lot looking for Tennessee. Chaos could be cold hearted and it bothered Petie. He always remembered that he had help on his journey, and helping others who needed help was his way of giving back. Petie had taken a lot from people and when he started to come to terms with his disease. He considered it his way of paying his dues.

Petie spotted Tennessee over by the Dunkin' Donuts so he got out of his truck telling Chaos, "I'll be right back." He walked over to Tennessee and told him, "Go inside." It was more like and order than a request.

They walked inside and Petie had a seat at one of the tables.

Tennessee sat down across from him. "Are you hungry?" Petie asked. Tennessee seemed to be put off by the question. He thought about it for a minute and then answered, "Yeah, I could go for something to eat".

Petie wasted no time in getting right to the point. He leaned back in his chair and asked Tennessee if he wanted to work. Tennessee answered quickly, "Yeah, partner I'd love a job. But you see I'm looking for something off the books."

Petie stared him down trying to figure Tennessee out. It wasn't hard to do. Petie concluded that he was on the run too. Petie understood being that New York was still looking for him. If it had not have been for Patrice's mother, he wouldn't have a whole new identity. "I got something for you to do that's off the books. It's not landscaping or plumbing work but it's off the books like you need it to be," Petie clarified.

He went into his pocket and took out a knot of money the size of a skinny chick's thigh. Petie peeled back three-hundred dollars and passed it to Tennessee across the table.

"Get yourself cleaned up. Buy some clothes, get a shave, and if you staying in the street then get a room somewhere for tonight. I'll come and get you tomorrow afternoon around one. Ya heard?" he instructed Tennessee and got up from the table.

Tennessee got up behind him and walked Petie to the door and then said, "Can I ask you something?"

"Nope, see you tomorrow," Petie replied, walking to his truck. Chaos grilled Tennessee from out the window as they pulled off.

"That's him?" Chaos asked as they pulled into traffic.

"Yeah, he's on the run. I gave the nigga some dough and told him to get his self fixed up. Tomorrow come pick him up at one and tell me what kind of vibes you get from him. Ya heard?"

"Yeah, if he ain't there I'm kill his ass next time we run across him," Chaos said stone faced.

They were silent for most of the ride back until Chaos asked, "what we gonna do wit' Country?"

"Get rid of him," Petie simply answered.

"Yeah, his time is up. We should've done that months ago when Josephine said she seen him smoking our shit. Big pork chop, and mashed potato eating muthafucka," Chaos said, referring to Country.

"Well, we don't need him anymore," Petie said, pulling into the back of the house.

He shut off the engine and then told Chaos that his oldest son was coming out from PA. tonight. Petie told him that he didn't know what he was going to do with Darnell because he was reckless. He didn't tell Chaos what Darnell had done because that wasn't Chaos' business, but he did tell him that Darnell was wilding out.

"Petie man, you know he been wanting to live out here with you for years. Shit, I remember a couple of times the nigga crying because he had to go back with his mother. He loves you to death. That nigga worship the ground that you walk on, anybody can see that," Chaos said, causing Petie to smile.

Darnell was crazy about his father. All the more reason Petie wouldn't let him walk in his shoes. If Darnell thought that he was coming down so that he could get in the game, well he had another thing coming. Petie was not having that at all. None of his sons would follow in his steps as long as he was alive. He wanted much more for them than what he had chosen for himself.

"Yeah, I know. That's my man," Petie said still smiling when he opened the door.

They went inside the house and Petie told Country to call

Dougie. He was a regular customer that came from Va. every month to cop. Country said that he had just spoken to Dougie a little while ago and that he was en route; he was less than an hour away.

"Good, is everything ready for him?" Petie asked, walking down to the basement.

"Yeah," Country answered.

Petie went to the back of the basement where he kept his vicious pit bulls at and let them out. He walked with them up the stairs to take them outside. Chaos came outside with Petie and the two of them sat on the steps while the dogs ran around the front yard. Chaos said, "So, I think we should get rid of this nigga this week." Petie looked into his partner's cold blooded merciless eyes.

"This week…? Nah, we gettin' rid of him tonight," Petie said.

ƆHAPTER ꓝOURTEEN
ꟼENNSYLVANIA

Renee had just set Darnell's last bag at the door when she heard the car pull up. She looked out the window to see him getting out of a car. Rodney, she thought. She opened the door and let Darnell walk past her into the house.

"Did you speak to your father?" she asked.

"Yes," he said politely.

Renee looked at him as he walked to the kitchen wondering why he couldn't always be that polite and respectful. Only Petie could get him to show respect and that made her feel less than a mother. She remembered when she and Darnell were friends. What happened? She wondered while watching him pour soda into a glass.

"Darnell, I want to talk about what happened today," Renee said, walking into the kitchen.

She leaned against the counter and watched her oldest son while he drank his soda. She wanted to see if he showed any expressions of regret before he answered.

"I'm listening, mom," Darnell said putting his cup in the sink.

"Darnell, why'd you do that? Just tell me, why?"

"I don't know. I think she be cheating on Donte and I wanted to see for myself. Most of them chicks are ho's and Donte is a snowflake. So he would never know if she was gaming him or not," he explained, trying to justify what he had done.

"So, you were protecting Donte? Is that what you're telling me?" Renee asked, not believing a word he was saying.

"Yeah, in a way I was," Darnell answered, walking out of the kitchen.

Renee didn't have a chance to ask him another question because Donte came in. He set his athletic bag on the floor and without saying a word he tackled Darnell in the middle of the floor. "Muthafucka, I'm going to kill you!" Donte yelled, punching Darnell everywhere.

"Stop it!" Renee screamed while the two brothers rolled around on the floor.

Darnell flipped Donte over and head butted him. It had no effect because Donte jumped up and punched Darnell in the jaw. Darnell staggered, grabbed Donte by the throat, and kneed him in the stomach.

"Goddammit! That's enough!" Renee screamed, trying to get in between them.

Donte fell to the floor and Darnell jumped on him punching him in the head yelling, "You faggot ass punk! You can't beat me!"

Renee jumped on Darnell's back pulling him off Donte screaming, "That's enough! I said stop it, goddammit!"

Darnell fell backwards. Donte scrambled to his feet, and put his knee in Darnell's throat, hitting him with ferocious blows.

"I hate you!" Donte screamed at the top of his lungs while beating up his big brother. "I swear to God I hate you!"

Darnell couldn't get up because Donte was holding him down with his knee in his throat. Darnell could not breathe. Renee could see him gasping for air and she grabbed the back of Donte's NBA shirt and pulled him off of Darnell.

"Go to your room, now!" she yelled pointing at Donte. "I said now goddammit!"

Darnell was on the floor choking trying to catch his breath.

"I'm gonna kill him, mom. I swear to God I'm gonna kill his ass!" Donte yelled, stomping up the steps.

Darnell got up and snatched off his shirt ready to fight again. He had blood coming from his nose and the top of his lip.

"I'm fucking you up punk!" he yelled at Donte.

"Get over there and sit down now!"

"No fuck that! I'm fucking him up! I don't care what you say," Darnell said, pacing back and forth.

"Darnell, sit down. It's over with. Sit the fuck down! You started this shit! How do you expect him to feel, huh? You did this not him. You need to be mad at you and not Donte. That's his girlfriend and you had no right doing what you did," Renee said, standing in front of Darnell.

"I don't care. He snuffed me and I'm gonna get his ass," Darnell said, trying to push pass Renee.

She told him, "Boy if you hit me, I'll bury you. Now I said sit the fuck down."

Darnell flopped on the couch, and wiped the blood from his nose then rubbed it on his jeans. Renee stood staring at him wondering. She didn't know her son anymore. He was totally foreign to her these past few years. She never knew that he had such a troubled mind. Darnell got up and flipped the coffee table over and stormed out of the front door. The vases shattered in pieces and the flower arrangement flew all over the living room. She stepped over the mess and picked up the phone to call Amtrak. Darnell had to get out of her house no sooner than immediately. To top her day off she still had not spoken to Cliff about his son's crime-spree. Renee folded her arms, looked around the disheveled room with her thoughts in a shamble.

Cliff had been in a meeting with one of his clients all day. When he got back his secretary told him that his son had been calling all day.

"Why didn't you beep me?" he asked.

"I did sir, but you didn't call back," she said, gazing at him with concern. "I think he's in some kind of trouble he, uh…well he said he couldn't leave a number and that they weren't going to let him call again," she explained.

"Who is 'they', do you know?" Cliff asked.

"Sir, I have no idea but I would think that he's been arrested," she said.

"No, I don't think that's possible. I'll be in my office for about another…" Cliff looked at his watch and continued. "Twenty minutes or so… any calls just put it through."

Cliff walked to his office, closed the door behind him and flopped on the sofa that he had in the corner. He rubbed his temples trying to ease the headache, threatening. Feeling uneasy by what his secretary had told him, he checked his voicemail to see if Calvin had called. Cliff listened to four messages and the fifth was from Calvin.

He was at the municipal building on MacDade Boulevard being held for questioning. That's what he said on the message but he didn't mention what had really happened. Cliff jumped up from his desk and ran out of the office. He jumped in his car and sped out of the parking lot. Cliff raced to the municipal building and made a wild turn into the entrance. He slammed on the brakes, parked and jumped out leaving the keys in the ignition.

Cliff ran into the building and after identifying himself, he demanded to know where his son was.

"Have a seat and someone will be out to talk to you," he was told by an officer.

"I don't want to have a seat. I want to know where my son is, and why he's here," Cliff said firmly and aggressively.

The officer got up out of his seat and said, "Listen mister, you need to have a seat or else you'll be joining your son in the cell. Now, I said someone will be right out and that's that."

Cliff had a seat in the waiting area and watched while the officer picked up the telephone then spoke briefly. When he was through, he cut his eye at Cliff, smirked at him before he hung up. Cliff shifted in his seat, crossed his legs, and waited. Half hour later, an officer came out from behind closed doors.

"Are you Calvin Houser's father?" he asked.

Cliff got to his feet immediately and answered, "Yes, I am. What's going on? Why is my son being held here?"

"Your son is being held on several criminal felonies. At this time we're charging him with four counts of auto theft, endangering public safety, eluding law enforcement, resisting arrest, and a number of traffic violations," the officer deadpanned.

Cliff's mouth dropped open as the officer read off Calvin's charges. He was dumbfounded.

"There's got to be some kind of mistake. Can I see my son to make sure that you have the right individual? For all I know you've got the wrong person," Cliff said unconvinced that Calvin was in custody.

He was never in trouble in school. Cliff was sure that someone had to be impersonating his son.

"Wait here a minute," the officer said and walked back through the doors.

Cliff paced until the officer returned, showing him Calvin's mug shot picture straight off the computer.

"Is this your son?"

Cliff snatched the picture and still in denial he said, "There's got to be some kind of mistake."

"Is this your son?" the officer asked again.

"Yes, but…" Cliff was saying when the officer took the picture back.

"We're charging the right individual. You see your son was involved in a high-speed chase this morning that subsequently led to his arrest. We've reason to believe that he's also responsible for auto thefts in the surrounding Delaware County area."

"Can I see him, please," Cliff asked.

"No I can't allow that. I can tell you that he'll be seeing the judge in Media Courthouse and most likely he'll be transported to the county jail."

Cliff could not believe what he was hearing. There was nothing that he could say so he just turned and left the municipal building and went to his illegally parked car.

"Great," he said, snatching the ticket off the windshield, and getting into his car.

Devastated, he couldn't wait to see Renee. Seeing her would provide him some comfort. Cliff called her at home. He had to see her without going into details. Renee told him to come right over.

"Train schedules? Where's Darnell going?" Cliff asked, stopping for a stop sign.

"To his father… I can't deal with him anymore. I'll tell you everything when you get here," Renee said, sighing in exasperation.

"Is everything alright?" Cliff asked.

"No, actually it's not. There's a lot going on with…just everything. I need to tell you what happened this morning, Cliff. I'll wait for you to get here," Renee said, picking up the broken shards from the vases.

CHAPTER FIFTEEN
NEW YORK

A few days later, Venus was still in a coma, and showed no signs of coming out of it. Share stood by her bedside talking. Letting her know that she had changed the locks and had packed up Andre's belongings, and thrown them out, she laughed. She told Venus how Andre called threatening her with illegal eviction.

"It's not illegal because your name is not on any of my leases. As far as I'm concerned you're trespassing. Now don't call me anymore, and stay off my property," Share had told him.

Share went to the hospital everyday and talked to Venus. She had long one-way conversations with her best friend and read to her sometimes. Share wanted Venus to show some signs of life.

Time came when Share had to go. She kissed Venus' forehead and said, "I'll see you tomorrow, sista. I love you."

Share left the hospital quietly and got in her car. She was tired and anxious for tomorrow to come. Andre had a court appearance and Share prayed that the judge would revoke his bail. She wanted him to suffer like Venus did. Share was going to ruin him and his career. She wanted to wait and see how his court appearance went.

Share drove to the courthouse on 161st Street to meet with the District Attorney. She took the elevator up to the fourth floor and walked into the office. Share introduced herself and was happy to see that the D.A. was a round woman with red curly hair, a face too small for her body, and intelligent eyes. She was dressed like a schoolteacher and looked over her glasses at Share and asked, "What can I do for you, Miss Jacobs?"

"I'm concerned about the charges against Andre Daniels.

He's only being charged with assault and battery correct?" Share said, sitting down.

The district attorney reached for a file and after looking through it she said, "That is correct."

She closed the file and looked at Share waiting for her to finish.

Share continued, "Are you aware that Venus Wilkins is in a coma? She has an aneurysm and her frontal lobe was so swelled that the doctors had to be extra careful in treating her. This man tried to kill her. I think that assault and battery charge is an outrage compared to what he has done to her. She is still showing no signs of movement and the doctors don't know when she will come out of the coma that Andre beat her in to."

Share stopped to let what she said sink in. She could see the devastation registering on the D.A.'s face. She obviously didn't know that it was that severe.

After a moment the D.A. said, "I will discuss this new information with my assistant who will be in court tomorrow handling this case. I want to thank you for coming. I had no idea. I've read the report and noticed that the police charged him with these counts. But I had no idea it was a domestic violence case. That of course will change everything. As I said I will speak to my assistant and I'll see if we can do better than what he's being charged with."

Share was satisfied. She got up and shook the woman's hand, thanking her. On her way out, she called Will to tell him that she was going to Venus' place to check on things. She didn't trust Andre and she thought maybe that he would try to break in or do something to her building. He had been furious when he had called her threatening and yelling all kind of obscenities.

She pulled up in front of her brownstone, and parked across

the street. Using the door on the second floor, Share went in and knocked on her tenant's door. A girl answered smiling. Share told her tenant that Venus was away and that she would be by to collect the rent.

"Oh, okay," the young woman said.

Share walked down the hall to the other apartment. She told the tenant there the same thing then she went upstairs. Share's tenants on the third floor were not home so she went downstairs to Venus' apartment. She entered the first floor apartment and stood in the living room, wondering what Venus had endured. The dogs greeted her by jumping up and down wanting to her to pet them.

"I know guys," Share said, petting them. "I miss her too."

She got on her knees, and the dogs licked her face. Share went into the kitchen and filled their bowls up with fresh food and water. They were hungry and lonely too. Share was entering Venus' room when warm air blew pass her. Share stopped and looked behind her. She had closed the door and wandered where the breeze was coming from.

The dogs stopped eating and started barking. They were looking at something. She shook the feeling off and walked into Venus' room and sat on the bed. Share put her head in her hands and wept. She would die if Venus didn't make it. She couldn't live without her best friend. Venus and Will were everything to her. It was Venus who had talked Share into buying her first McDonald's restaurant. Venus was the one who said, "Girl you got money, you better buy some property and get more money."

Share didn't think that she would be a good businesswoman and Venus pushed her when Share didn't believe in herself.

"God, please let her be okay. You know I need her Lord," Share cried and said a quiet prayer.

The dogs were still barking and now they were jumping around in the kitchen. Share got up and watched them. They were trying to grab at something. Whatever it was, it was coming closer to Share. The dogs were going crazy; jumping in the air and trying to grab a hold of something unseen to Share.

"What the hell is wrong?" she said out loud to Bullet and Diamond.

They were walking back towards the living room like they were following somebody or something. A strong breeze came through the living room, blowing the curtains around. She followed the dogs to the window, trying to see what they saw.

Finally, they sat down by the couch like nothing had happened. Share got their leashes and decided to take them home with her. Maybe they were going crazy being alone. She picked her pocket book up off the table and that's when she seen it. It was an old picture of her, Venus, and Porscha. Porscha was Share's second best friend who five years ago had died of an overdose in her apartment building.

Porscha and Petie's niece were lovers at the time. Back then tensions were high, and blood was bad between them. Petie's niece had gone on a rampage when she had found out that Will and his peeps had beaten Petie up so badly, he was hospitalized for weeks. Porscha could not deal with the strain that it put on their relationship. She suffered a relapse that took her life.

In the upstairs apartment that Porscha used to live, Venus found her body. Tears came to her eyes as she looked at the picture they had taken five years now. She understood why the dogs had been barking. Porscha's spirit came to visit that was why they were jumping in the air. They had seen Porscha. Share looked around in disbelief. That was the only way the photo could have gotten there.

Share put the leashes on the dog and opened the door. Share let them out, turned off the lights, and closed the foyer door. The warm breeze was still blowing with vigor, just like the same one she felt earlier. A smile creased her lips as she closed the outer door and locked it. The dogs looked back through the window as if they were looking at someone who was still there.

She put the dogs in the backseat and got in the car. The engine purred when she started it. Share looked back and that the light in the living room was back on. She knew she had turned it off. She stared at the living room window expecting someone to be there. Share smiled and slowly pulled off. Maybe her friend's spirit was trying to tell her something.

CHAPTER SIXTEEN
BALTIMORE, MARYLAND

Petie closed the front door and went outside to his truck. Darnell was waiting for him in the front seat talking to Renee on his cellphone. Amir was tucked tightly in the backseat.

"Yeah, mom… I know that already, you told me yesterday. Yeah, I love you I just want to be with dad. Why you taking it so personal…? Yeah, here talk to dad he's right here."

Darnell passed the phone to Petie as he got in the driver's seat. Petie took it and spoke briefly before ending the call. He passed the phone to Darnell, and started the truck.

"Where are we going, dad?" Darnell asked, buckling his seat belt.

"I want to go and check on something with my man. He got a job lined up for you and its good paying work. He's gonna look out, on my strength. I expect you to do the right thing."

"What kind of work is it?" Darnell asked, rolling his eyes.

"Construction, landscaping, painting…he owns the construction company, and he's good peeps. He's a white boy who thinks he's black. His girl is black, his music is black, his team at work and after work is black, nigga even drive a black truck," Petie said.

"Ahight, I'm wit' it. So when do I start?" Darnell asked, rubbing his hands together.

Petie looked over at his oldest son and smiled at him. He asked him why he couldn't be so willing when he was with Renee.

"I don't know, dad. She's just funny. She won't let a nigga grow up. She wants to give me an early curfew and she expects me to be like Donte. He's a snowflake and he acts like a wuss. The nigga always want to study and do his homework like a good little boy or some shit. I felt trapped out there, dad," Darnell explained slowly and with emotion.

Petie believed what he was saying. Renee was guilty of what Darnell had said, but that made her an even better mother as far as Petie was concerned. Darnell was just a rebel. The values Renee was instilling in him were corny.

"Yeah, well your mother wants you to have some structure and substance in your life. She wants you to go places and to achieve things that I didn't do or that she didn't do," Petie said, defending Renee.

"I know dad, but I feel like she trying to punk me sometimes. I'm not built like Donte. I'm built like you," Darnell said.

They pulled into the parking lot of the construction site. Petie got out and told Darnell to wait until he came back. Darnell watched his father go in the office. Ten minutes later he returned with a stocky, body building guy. He had dirty blond hair, with thin sideburns on his face and dark blue eyes.

Darnell got out of the truck and met them halfway. Petie said, "Darnell this is Greg. 'G' this is my oldest son."

"What's up?" Greg said and he gave Darnell a pound. "You ready to work?" he asked Darnell.

"Yeah, of course," Darnell said, liking Greg already. He liked his swagger-even for a white boy. But he knew that his father didn't deal with anyone that wasn't thorough.

"Be here in the morning at six-thirty sharp. Construction boots on your feet, work gloves on your hands, and be ready to go," Greg told Darnell.

"Yeah, no doubt," Darnell said, nodding.

Petie walked with Greg back into the office. Darnell got in the truck feeling good. He knew he'd be better off living with his father. Petie waved at him walked into the office, and closed the door.

"Let me know if he gives you any problems. I doubt it if he will but just in case, please holla at me," Petie said, going in his inside pocket, and pulling out a sandwich bag with five grams of raw in it. He passed it to Greg, smiled and said, "Good looking out my dude. I appreciate it."

"Petie, man you know that's not necessary," Greg said but he still took the bag.

"It's all good, my dude. I'll drop him off in the morning and you get somebody to bring him home. He doesn't know his way around yet," Petie said, opening the office door.

Greg put the bag in his desk drawer, and walked with Petie back to the truck.

"Darnell, I'll see you in the morning bright and early," he waved as Petie pulled out of the parking lot.

"How do you feel?" he asked, following traffic.

"Good. I'm ready to start right now," Darnell said while they waited for the light to change.

"That's what I want to hear," Petie smiled.

They drove to the shopping center and stopped at FootLocker. Proud father and happy sons went inside. Petie looked at some sneakers for Amir and told Darnell to get some boots for work. Petie bought two pair of sneakers for Amir. Darnell tried on several different styles of boots. Black or brown, he couldn't make up his mind. Petie told him to get both. They left and went to Dairy Queen for ice cream.

"What kind of ice cream do you want?" Petie asked Darnell.

"I'll take Butter Pecan."

"Dad I want strawberry and vanilla," Amir chimed in.

"I know," Petie said, rubbing Amir's head.

"Get a booth in the back," Petie told Darnell.

Darnell and Amir walked to the back. They sat in a booth by the window, facing the parking lot. There was a woman and a girl sitting in another booth across from them. Darnell immediately noticed the girl. She was pretty with long hair, braided past her shoulders. Darnell could not take his eyes off her. Petie sat down in the booth and gave them their ice cream.

"Amir, don't spill any on your shirt," he said.

"I won't dad," Amir answered.

Darnell ate his ice cream, his eyes still on the girl. Petie noticed and said, "Go say hello. What are you scared or something?"

Darnell smiled and then replied, "Of course not. Scared? Me? Picture that, dad."

"I can't tell. You can't even eat your ice cream you so busy watching her," Petie said.

"Yeah, whatever," Darnell said, and continued looking at her while eating his ice cream.

They talked about his new job and what Petie expected of him while he was out there with him. He let Darnell know that there would be no bullshitting around with this job.

"I expect you to take it seriously. I don't want my man, calling me telling me that you're not doing right," Petie said seriously.

"That's not going to happen, dad. I wanna work and I wanna stay out here. So you don't have to worry about that," Darnell said, focusing on his father.

The girl and the woman got up from the table and cleared their table. They were laughing at something when the girl looked Darnell's way. She smiled at him before leaving. That was all he needed. He got up quickly from the table and caught up with her before she got in the car.

"Excuse me, um how are you doing?" he asked, suddenly realizing he was at a loss for words. That never happened before.

"I'm fine," she said.

"Felicia, let's go," the woman called out from behind the wheel.

"I'm coming, mom," Felicia said.

"My name is Darnell," he said holding out his hand.

She took his hand in hers and smiled, "Nice to meet you. I'm Felicia".

"I just moved out here from PA., and I don't know anyone out here. I was hoping that... Well maybe we could go see a movie or something," Darnell said shyly.

"That would be real neat. Meet me here tomorrow around the same time, okay," she said, reaching for the car door handle. Darnell looked through the window and waved at her mother.

"How you doing?" she responded, starting the car.

"Okay. Well have a good day," Darnell said.

He went back inside the Dairy Queen, and sat down in front of his melting ice cream. Petie smiled at him, and took a bite of his sugar cone.

"So did you get the number?"

"Nah, she said to meet her back here tomorrow around this time," Darnell said, scooping ice cream in his mouth.

"How are you going to do that when you'll be at work?" Petie asked.

"Oh, I forgot," Darnell said, looking out the window.

Petie looked at his watch and then said, "Don't worry. You'll be off by this time tomorrow. I'll bring you back here so you can meet up with her."

"Good looking out, dad."

"Yeah, when you learn your way around then you can drive yourself. I'll get you a car to get around in," Petie said and stood, ready to get up from the table.

Having spent time with his sons, it was time for Petie to get back to business.

CHAPTER SEVENTEEN
PENNSYLVANIA

Renee walked down the steps of the courthouse and got in her car. As much as she hated coming to court, she had to. She had tried to explain this to Cliff, but he had hung up the phone several times on her. The fact that his son was stealing cars didn't matter to Cliff. He blamed her for everything. It was all Renee's fault and at times she felt that way.

She pulled up in front of her house and sat behind the wheel thinking. There was too much happening at one time. First Darnell, then Donte's grades had dropped from A's to C's, and now she had to testify at a hearing against her lover's son. What next? Her thoughts kept coming as she opened the car door.

Renee dropped her bag on the sofa and flopped onto the cushions. She was so frustrated and overwhelmed by everything going on. She felt so alone it was scary.

Adding to the gloom she already felt, raindrops started beating against the window. Renee got up and closed the windows then did the same in the kitchen. She wanted to talk to someone, anyone that would listen. Donte was at school and Cliff wasn't speaking to her. Renee called one of the ladies from the support group.

After speaking for nearly an hour, Renee hung up, and went upstairs to get in the shower. That would take some tension off of her for sure, she thought. Lonely and empty was how she felt while the steaming hot water beat on her back. She wondered how Darnell was doing. She had not heard from him or Petie in three days. No news must be good news she thought while lathering up with soap.

Cliff left the courthouse shortly after Renee. He sat in his car until it started raining. This was his cue to get home before it got worse. He drove for a short distance, and pulled over to the side of the road. Cliff banged his fist on the steering wheel in frustration. Bail had not been set for Calvin, and Cliff thought the judge was prejudiced. He made it seem as if Calvin had killed people. For crying out loud he stole a few cars. What's the big deal? Cliff's thoughts were in extra gear. Then his thoughts turned to Renee. What the hell had she been doing that morning? Playing Wonder Woman behind the wheel? Why didn't she just mind her business? None of this would be happening if she would have just went to work, and minded her own goddamn business.

He drove by her block on his way home and stopped in front of her house. Cliff sat in the car for a moment then marched up to the front door. He used the key that he had and let himself in. He could hear the shower upstairs running. Cliff took off his jacket and went in the kitchen and fixed a drink. He waited until the water stopped. He quickly downed his drink and went upstairs. Renee was just coming out of the bathroom when she seen him on the steps. She jumped.

"What are you doing here? You treat me like this is my fault, and then you sneak in my house?" She asked, walking to her bedroom with Cliff right behind her.

"Do you know that thanks to you my son is not getting bail?"

"Thanks to me...? You can't be serious!" Renee repeated. "No try thanks to him," she turned her back and started to dry with a towel.

"What are you trying to prove here, Renee? You want recognition for something is that what it is?" Cliff asked, walking towards her.

Renee sat on the bed and took a deep breath before letting

him have it.

"You listen to me, dammit. I wasn't the one stealing cars at the convenience store. And then racing down the pike with every cop car available chasing me! I just so happened to be there, Cliff. I didn't know it was Calvin behind the wheel. I wish I would have taken a different route that morning, but I didn't. What the hell do you want from me?"

"How about a little loyalty…? Is that asking too much?" Cliff got up in her face and shouted. His light skinned face was turning red.

"Loyalty…? What the hell am I supposed to do? Tell the judge that I was hallucinating when I called 911 and that everything I witnessed was in my imagination? Don't' you dare blame me! You blame Calvin for his actions not me. Now get out of my house!" Renee said, jumping up from the bed.

"You realize that you've turned my love to nothing but hatred for you, don't you? You have ruined my son's life and yet you stand here like you've done nothing."

"I haven't done anything, Cliff. Why can't you see that?" Renee said, her eyes pleading for some kind of understanding.

Cliff stared at her for minutes before he threw the keys on the bed and stomped out. She stood there and listened to the door slam before she broke down in tears.

CHAPTER EIGHTEEN
BALTIMORE, MARYLAND

Sunlight reverberated off the building with the brilliance of diamonds. Petie sat outside the motel waiting for Tennessee to come out. Petie had been on the phone with Ladelle, his old partner and long time friend. Tennessee had been working for Petie for a few weeks, and so far so good. Chaos had even gotten used to Tennessee but still kept a watchful eye on him around the money and material. Tennessee came out of the motel room. He had a look of ease about him. Petie noticed as he hopped in the truck.

"What's up partner?" he said pulling the door closed.

Partner, Petie thought looking at him sideways.

"Don't worry about it," Petie said, pulling out of the motel parking lot. "We got a lot of work to do this week. First, we gotta get you a place besides this motel."

"Yeah, the maids are starting to look at me funny. I don't want to open the door one morning to any surprises," Tennessee said, putting on his seatbelt. He looked over at Petie and said, "You know what I mean, right?"

"Of course," Petie said, knowing all too well what was meant.

They pulled up to the shack, and Tennessee got out. Petie drove the truck around back and into the garage. The dogs were tied up and they barked and jumped trying to get loose when they saw him. He let his meanest dog, named after him loose. The dog followed Petie at his heels.

Tupac's *Life Goes On,* blared from the speakers. Chaos was at the table cutting coke when Petie entered. He looked up from what he was doing and said, "This nigga Doug called and said he was coming through. He said that other package moved so quick that he needs more."

Petie sat down and asked, "What he wants this time?"

"Fifty…"

"Get that ready," Petie told Tennessee who was standing in the doorway.

Tennessee went to the back room. He unlocked the door to the safe where the kilos were stacked in the floor. He went into another small room and took out the electronic scale and weighed out fifty grams of pure fish scales. He took it off the scale, ten grams at a time, and packaged it before taking it out to Petie.

"When are they coming?" Tennessee asked, handing the weight to Petie.

Chaos looked at his watch.

"Any minute now, he was crossing the bridge about an hour ago."

"He's driving?" Petie asked.

"I guess so. That's what it sounded like to me," Chaos said getting up from the table.

Chaos scooped up the raw on an album cover, and went to the same room Tennessee left. He took out two large Ziploc bags, and evened the raw in each. Chaos returned when he was satisfied. He entered the room and Petie's phone rang.

"Speak," Petie said, quickly checking the caller I.D. like he always do.

"I'm here," Dougie responded.

"Come through the back," Petie instructed.

He got up and before he could hit the back door his dog was trying to jump over the fence at Dougie. The other dogs were jumping and barking from their leashed chains. Petie swaggered to the gated fence.

"What took you so long? You crossed the bridge an hour ago and you just getting here?" Petie asked holding the dog.

Dougie and his man hesitated then walked cautiously. They were tentative while quietly being watched dog.

"Make sure you got him good," Dougie said.

"Don't worry about him, that's not your job. He's worried about you," Petie said, leading his meanest dog inside. Tennessee was waiting for them at the table.

"Open your jackets and turn around let me see your waist," Tennessee said as soon as Dougie and his partner got inside.

"You heard him. Open up y'all jackets," Petie said. "Meaning right now—not now…"

Dougie shot Petie a look of surprise, but opened his jacket and turned around. His man followed suit.

"What's this about?" Dougie asked, looking at Petie.

"Precautions," Chaos answered in a cold tone.

"No problem," Dougie said, holding up his hands in surrender.

"If it's not a problem then why are you asking?" Petie said, rubbing his dog's head.

"Enough chit chat," Chaos said, putting the packaged raw for Dougie on the scale.

He weighed it out and set it back on the table in front of Petie. Dougie went inside his jacket pocket and pulled out fifteen-hundred dollars and passed it to Chaos, who then passed it to Petie. Petie counted the money before passing the package to Dougie. He got up and walked them to the back door.

Dougie asked, "Where's Country?"

"Missing," Petie replied, opening the gate for them.

"Oh word?" Dougie said, leaving out the gate. "I never really trusted his ass you know that, right?"

"I don't know anything," Petie answered with sarcasm.

He closed the gate. Petie wasn't for the small talk from anybody. Cop and bop, my dude, he thought watching them until they pulled off. It wasn't necessary for him to tell Dougie that Chaos had shot Country and then cut him up with a chain saw.

Dougie pulled over at a rest stop off the freeway. He and his partner got out to use the restroom and then get some chicken from KFC. They did not notice the two Impalas that had been following them since they crossed over Washington State lines. When the agents stopped them as they were getting into the car it was a bitter surprise.

"Put your hands up where I can see 'em!" an agent ordered, holding heat.

Two other agents jumped from another car. Dougie dropped his fast food and put his hands up. His partner took off sprinting through the parking lot. Another car pulled into action and chased him, nearly running him down. He jumped over the hood and kept running. Dougie was thrown against the car and handcuffed immediately.

"What did I do?" he whined like a schoolboy.

"Just take it easy, guy. Just relax," the agent answered,

handcuffing him.

They caught up with his partner and threw him to the ground. Dougie looked over and he could see his partner still putting up a fight from the ground. He was putting in work on them until they started stomping him repeatedly. He was brought back to the car in handcuffs; his shirt torn and tattered, and he was bleeding from his mouth and ear.

"Oh God…!" Dougie moaned like he was hit by a blow.

He turned and saw other agents quickly arriving on the scene. Soon they were surrounded by a wall of federal agents.

"Look I don't' know him. He picked me up on the road," Dougie squealed.

"Shaddup asshole. Just shut your trap, buddy!" One of the other agents barked, cutting him off.

"Got anything in your pockets that may stick me? Any needles, razors…?" another agent asked Dougie while patting him down.

"No, no I don't know anything," he said.

"Before you start lying, give us the chance to ask the questions, asshole," another agent interjected.

Dougie put his head down and shook it from side to side. They put his partner in the back seat of one of the Impalas and then put Dougie in another.

The agents poured over the car Dougie and his partner had been traveling in. Dougie watched from the backseat while they pulled the bags out from underneath the seat. He strained his ear to hear what they were saying. He could see one of them putting their find in a manila envelope. Then he wrote something on it before passing it to another agent. Dougie's mind raced against time. He knew they were going down unless.

At the police headquarters, Dougie and his partner were placed in separate rooms. Dougie was handcuffed to the chair in a room with two-way mirror. He could feel eyes on him knowing that they were there.

"Can I use the bathroom?" he called out.

Moments later the door opened and two agents walked in. They sat across from him.

"Where were you coming from?" one asked.

"North Carolina," Dougie said looking at them with hope in his eyes. "Listen…I was hitchhiking and that guy picked me up…"

The second agent cut him off waving his hand saying, "Listen, pal stop with the bullshit. We've been following you since Washington. Now, you're not going to waste our time here are you?"

"You know what we found in the car? So let's be straight up with each other. You help us and we help you," the first agent added.

Dougie felt an impulse rush from his foot to his brain. He wanted to get up and run, but where was he going handcuffed to a metal table?

"I don't know it must have been the guy's. I didn't even know there were drugs in the car," Dougie said with a straight face.

"Who said anything about drugs?" the first agent said, looking at his partner. He asked him, "Did you say we found drugs in the car?"

His partner shook his head, "Nope, not me."

The first agent turned back to Dougie and said, "What I said was, 'you know what we found in the car'. I never mentioned drugs."

He stared at Dougie; no wink not even a half smile. The second agent pushed back his chair causing it to scrape the floor.

"Let's get out of here. I'll start the paperwork on him. We got him for trafficking, distribution, and whatever else I can think of."

"Sounds fair to me," the first one said getting up.

"Wait, I don't know much but I can tell you what I do know," Dougie said.

The agents sat back down and the second one said, "Talk, and don't waste my fucking time."

"Well, it's this guy. I know him only as Petie…"

In the other interrogation room, Dougie's partner sat at a similar table handcuffed, his feet shackled to the floor restraints. Agents had come in and tried to get info from him and all he had to say was, "Fuck y'all! Suck my dick, I ain't telling you shit!"

"Well your friend says that the drugs are yours," one of them lied. "He says that you're the boss of everything. So I guess since you're not cooperating, we'll just charge you with everything and let your friend go. How's that sound?"

"Do what the fuck you wanna do. Just give me my phone call that I'm entitled to," Dougie's partner said not feeding into what they were saying.

"Have it your way, pal," the agent said, leaving the room and slamming the door.

ЭHAPTER ИINETEEN
ИEW YORK

Andre left the courthouse and headed straight to work. He had another court appearance next month. He could still see the cold look that Share had given him as he walked out of the courthouse. That fucking bitch, he thought. He got to work and immediately he was called to the main branch office. When he arrived the executive wasted no time.

"Mr. Daniels it has been the board's decision to suspend you indefinitely until your, uh, court case is over. We think that your current criminal situation is bad publicity for the bank. And its best if you keep a low profile for the bank's reputation."

"Are you kidding me?" Andre responded incredulously. "After all I've done for this bank, and you're telling me that you're worried about reputation…?"

"That's right. It's been brought to my attention that you are being charged with felonious assault. You told us you were involved in fighting a traffic ticket," the executive explained, sitting back smug behind his big desk. He tented his hands in front of him, watching Andre squirming.

"Brought to your attention, by whom? Tell me?" Andre demanded.

"Now, now, that is not the issue here. The issue is that we, meaning the bank, do not need that kind of publicity. Nevertheless, the board's decision is final. Your position is not being terminated, pending the outcome of the case of course. We just don't want any unneeded attention, you understand? Now you go on home and get yourself some rest. Think of it as a short vacation."

Andre stormed out of his office and back to his bank. He cleaned out his desk. Andre did not want the other employees to see him, and left the bank out the side door. He drove to the hotel where he had been staying in midtown, carried the stuff from his office up the steps to the third floor to his room. In the hallway he asked the maid, "Did you change my sheets yet?"

"Not yet. I have not gotten to your room yet," she said, pushing her cleaning cart down the hall.

Andre opened the door with his card and walked in. He put the box down and removed his jacket, hanging it in the closet. Andre flopped on his back, staring at the ceiling fan spin. The light breeze felt good on his forehead. Andre started drifting off to another place and time.

He was fifteen again. It was a sunny day, and hot as hell. Andre sat on the grass waiting for his girlfriend, Suzie to arrive. They were having a picnic and Andre was hoping that she would hurry up because he was getting hungry. He knew that she had to sneak to see him. Her father forbade her to go out with boys.

She arrived carrying a basket in one hand and her pocketbook in the other. Andre hated that pocketbook. It looked like a bag that an old woman would carry. It was old-fashioned with a lot of flowers on it, and way too big. She sat down on the grass and leaned in to give Andre a kiss. She put her arms around his neck and pulled him closer to her. Their lips locked for several minutes before they broke for air. She was on her back in the grass waiting for more, but Andre ignored her.

"What took you so long?" he asked, lifting the top off of the basket.

She twirled her hair between her fingers and said, "I was getting ready...for you."

She winked her eye at Andre and ran her tongue slowly over her lips. He turned his head away ignoring her.

She was loose. His mother had always warned him of girls like her. She wanted him to take her, but he wouldn't. She was no-good, a slut. Ugly thoughts spun tightened Andre as he reached for the sandwiches in the basket. She was on her feet standing behind him and rubbing his manhood. He turned around and passed her a sandwich.

"Here, let's eat."

He took out another sandwich and bit into it while she nibbled on his neck. Andre could feel his manhood rising. He felt the sweat on his brow and the tightness in his chest. She had better stop this or else.

"Let's eat later," she whispered with her tongue in his ear.

Andre dropped his sandwich on the grass and turned toward her. A quick glance around him, and he was on her, pushing her down. She laughed in a joking way throwing her head back against the short lades of the grass.

Oh it's funny...? The thought seeped into him and filled his mind like muck in a swamp. He uncontrollably jumped on her, and wrapped his hands around the softness of her neck. Then Andre squeezed as hard as he could, feeling the tension growing in his chest as her eyes rolled back in her head. She kicked and tried grabbing him. All of a sudden she stopped moving. Andre's heart pounded against his ribcage as he stared into her hollow, lifeless eyes. He picked her up and carried her to the edge of the water. Then he went back to get her granny bag that he hated so much. Andre put the bag around her neck, filling it with rocks. He then dragged her body into *the water and watched her sink. He took the basket and did the same thing with it. Andre wiped the sweat off his face. Rest in peace my dear with the fishes, he wanted to say. But his lips were dry.*

The knock at the door brought Andre out of his thoughts. He jumped off the bed sweaty, his heart beating like a scared rabbit.

"Who's there?"

"Housekeeping," the voice shouted through the door.

"One moment," Andre said grabbing a towel out of the bathroom. He wiped his face and chest quickly before opening the door.

"What is it?" he said swinging the door open with the towel draped around his shoulders. She stepped back with confusion on her face.

"I thought you wanted your room cleaned," she said looking pass him.

"No, just lemme have some clean sheets," Andre said and went back in the room. He stripped the bed of the linen. "Here," he said passing them to her.

"What about your towels?" she asked, putting the old sheets in a cart. She gave him a clean set.

"Oh yeah," Andre said, handing her the one around his neck.

He walked away to get the other towels. She was left standing in the doorway and the door closed in her face. She stared at the door shaking her head as the door opened.

"Here you go," Andre said, tossing the towel in her cart, and took the two that she offered. "Thanks," he said closing the door.

CHAPTER TWENTY
NEW YORK

On seeing the familiar number, Lydia answered her cellphone immediately.

"Hello," she said quietly.

"Yes, hell is low," the caller chuckled.

"Ha, ha, what's up? I'm in the restaurant. Your timing really sucks," she said, looking around to make sure that Ladelle was not coming. "Where are you anyway?" she asked closing the office door.

"At our spot, where else would I be?"

"You can be anywhere," she said laughing. "I'll be there in an hour. Just wait for me, okay?"

"Are you telling me or asking me?"

"Both. See you in an hour," Lydia said quickly ending the call.

Ladelle came in the office minutes later and told Lydia that he had somewhere to go and would be back as soon as he could.

"Um, alright I have to step out also. What time are you coming back?" she asked.

Her man looked at his watch and said, "Thirty, forty-five minutes tops."

She stood up and kissed him, twirling her tongue around in his mouth. Ladelle pulled away and held her in his arms. "I love you, you do know that, don't you?" he said in her ear.

"Yes, I do," Lydia said softly.

"I'll see you when I get back."

He walked up the stairs to the main floor. Ladelle told the manager on duty he would be returning shortly. He left and dashed to his car. Ladelle drove to Central Park, not far from where he lived. He sat in his car and waited. The person he was meeting quickly made his way to the car. Ladelle hit the button and his passenger got in.

"How you doing on this fine day?" the man asked, closing the door.

"I'm as good as can be expected," Ladelle answered. "What have you got for me, Bobby?"

Ladelle was meeting with an old friend who specialized in private investigating. Ladelle had asked him to follow Lydia because he suspected her of cheating. Bobby was delivering what he had uncovered.

"Well," Bobby started out, pulling a folder out of his inner pocket. "I got what you asked for. I was really hoping that you were wrong but you weren't." He handed the folder to Ladelle and said, "Here you go."

Ladelle took a deep breath and opened the folder. He removed the pictures inside. They were clear shots from different angles showing Lydia going in, and coming out of the same hotel on a number of occasions. Ladelle sighed as he viewed through the photos one by one. He put the pictures back in the folder and placed the folder under the seat.

"She's going out again today. Follow her and see if you can get a picture of her with someone. That'll stand up in court when I file for sole custody," he said showing no emotion.

"I've been trying to do that but she always goes right to the elevator. It's not like she meets someone in the lobby so it's kind of difficult brotha. I'll give it a shot. If I find out what room she goes to, I could get a name of the person. But as of now she's very careful.

And as you can see she's in and out," Bobby explained.

"Alright, just do what you can. I gotta get back because she's waiting for me. Maybe, you can catch her today with something a little more solid," Ladelle said, starting the car.

"I will brotha, and I'm sorry you had to find out like this. I'll do what I can."

Ladelle drove back to the restaurant. He didn't want to hold up Lydia from her rendezvous. Ladelle parked around the back and entered his restaurant from the back door, through the kitchen. He stopped and had a few polite words for the cooks, cracked a few jokes, and walked around the side to the office.

Lydia was busying herself at the computer. She turned when Ladelle came in and got off the computer.

"Oh, that was quick," she said, picking her handbag up off the computer table.

"Yeah," Ladelle deadpanned, turning his back and opening up a file cabinet drawer.

There wasn't anything else he could think of doing. What do you do when you find out that the woman you love is cheating on you? He pondered, staring aimlessly into the drawer. He coughed when Lydia leaned in trying to kiss him.

"Are you catching a cold, baby?" she asked, looking concerned. "Because if you are you know the kitchen is off limits for you."

"I'll be fine," Ladelle said.

He kissed her on the cheek so she wouldn't be suspicious. Ladelle walked her to the door.

"I'll be back as soon as I can, baby," Lydia said, walking out the office door.

"Take your time," Ladelle said, disgust registered on his grill.

He waited a few minutes before dialing rapidly on his cellphone. Bobby answered the phone saying, "I see her. I'm on her brotha."

"Alright, call me later at home," Ladelle said.

After ending the call, he leaned on the file cabinet, rubbing his temples. He checked his watch to keep track of the time, knowing that he had to pick up Ladir from his mother's house soon. Ladelle went up the steps to the main area. He stopped at a few tables, and spoke with regulars having an early dinner then he made his way to the bar. At the table sat a regular who came in a few times a week. Ladelle spoke to her briefly then made his way to the back of the restaurant.

The woman called out to Ladelle, signaling for him to come to her table. Ladelle turned, and approached her table, smiling.

"Yes, what can I do for you?"

"You can have a drink with me," she smiled, showing perfect teeth.

"Well that would be nice, but unfortunately I cannot indulge you right now. I have a restaurant to run," Ladelle said.

"My name is Nadirah," she said, extending her hand.

Ladelle noticed that her nails weren't manicured, and that she didn't have a head full of phony hair. She was natural with a mane full of long dreadlocks, twisted down her back. She wore no lipstick or any kind of make-up. Ladelle was impressed and a little intimidated at the same time.

"I'm Ladelle," he said, taking her hand in his.

"Well, I'll take no for an answer now, but I won't after you close up," Nadirah said, twirling the ice around in her drink.

"Well in that case I guess I'll be having a drink with you," Ladelle said sheepishly. "I have some things to do now, but if you are still here, well then we'll be having that drink on the house," he added, walking to the back of the restaurant. What's good for the goose is better for the gander, he smiled.

CHAPTER TWENTY-ONE
BALTIMORE, MARYLAND

Darnell waited outside of the high school for Felicia to come out. He had been picking her up from school for the past week after he got off from work. They had been spending a lot of time together. Darnell really liked Felicia and was taking his time building a relationship with her. He spotted Felicia in a crowd of her peers. She was holding her backpack around her shoulder. Darnell planned on taking her home with him. He wanted her to meet his father. He felt a little excitement building at the prospects. He knew how Donte felt when he brought Sonya home to meet Renee. He never brought a chick home unless it was to bone her. One day he would kiss Felicia on the lips, not yet. Felicia was pure, Darnell knew. She was virgin material.

She saw Darnell leaning against the fence and waved. He smiled brightly. Felicia walked up to him and kissed Darnell on his cheek. He took her hand in his and kissed the back of it.

"How was your day?" he asked as they walked off of the school grounds. Darnell took her backpack and put it over his shoulder.

"Fine, how was yours?" she asked, looking at him. Her eyes conveyed more.

"It was long because I was thinking about you all day," Darnell said with sincerity.

"Yeah, right," she said, looking at him sharply with black diamond eyes.

"I'm dead serious," Darnell said. He stopped, stared in her eyes, and said, "No, I am so serious. I think about you day in and out.

I need you to know that, Felicia."

Felicia was blushing when Darnell cupped her face in his hands. He kissed her softly on her forehead. He felt something he had never felt before. Felicia was the one. He let his guard down. He wanted Felicia to know he trusted her.

"Do you have to go straight home?" he asked, hoping she would say no.

"You know that I do because my mom is going to be worried. Why?"

"I wanted us to stop by my crib and maybe watch some T.V. or something. You know eat and watch a movie on the big screen," Darnell shyly answered.

Felicia saw the anticipation build on Darnell's young, rugged face. His peach fuzz around his lips strained as she thought about his plans.

"Let me call my mom first and let her know first, okay," she said.

"Yeah," Darnell was sprung as he quickly passed her his cellphone.

Darnell watched as Felicia dialed her number. She spoke into the phone briefly before ending the call and giving Darnell back his phone.

"She said 'yes', but I gotta be home before seven."

"Alright, that's cool," Darnell said, pepping up his step.

They entered the house through the kitchen door. Patrice was busy making grilled chicken salad on the center island. She looked up when the door opened and said, "You scared me. Your father is the only one that uses the kitchen door and he's upstairs." She noticed Felicia and said, "You must be Felicia. Darnell talks about you all the time." Patrice winked at Darnell, and smiled.

"I'm Patrice," she said, wiping her hands on her apron over her very pregnant stomach. She held her hand out to Felicia.

"Please to meet you," Felicia said. "How many months are you?" Felicia smiled, looking at Patrice's stomach.

"Eight and counting," Patrice said, rubbing her stomach.

"Are you having a boy or a girl"?

"A girl, thank God. I couldn't deal with another boy," Patrice laughed.

"My father is upstairs, right?" Darnell asked Patrice.

"Yeah, he's in the gym," she said.

"Alright, we are going upstairs. We'll be back down for that tasty looking salad," Darnell said. To Felicia he said, "Come on."

Darnell gave Felicia a tour through the spacious six-bedroom house. He took her down to the basement that was an arcade. It had pinball machines, video games, a pool and Ping-Pong table.

"Your house is so nice, Darnell," she said.

They climbed the steps that overlooked the living room and stopped by the gym. Petie was working out and looked up. He put the weights down, and said to Darnell, "What's good? How was your day?"

"It was alright. Dad, you remember Felicia right?"

"You've been talking about her now for the longest. How can I forget her?"

Petie smiled at Felicia. She was blushing, showing her dimples.

"We're gonna watch a movie in my room before I take her home," Darnell said.

"Yeah, alright leave your bedroom door cracked, you heard?" Petie said.

"Yeah dad..."

Darnell's voice trailed as they walked down the carpeted hall to his room.

"It's a little messy," he said, opening the door.

"That's alright," Felicia said as they walked in.

She looked around the large room admiring his entertainment center covering one wall. His posters covered the other sides.

"I see you love Tupac too," she said, staring at the many posters of the slain and well-loved entertainer.

"Yeah, Tupac and Biggie, as far as I'm concerned they were both the best. The rap industry suffered when they died, you feel me? I'm gonna jump in the shower so you can pick out a movie that you want to see. I got everything on the shelf," he said, taking off his work boots.

Darnell looked over at Felicia, he told her to sit down and be comfortable. He removed a change of clothes from his closet. Felicia got up and looked through the movies before selecting *Platoon*. "I just love military movies. Do you have *Full Metal Jacket*?" she asked while turning on the DVD player.

"Yeah, it's probably in the back. Take a look while I get in the shower," Darnell said, putting his clothes over his arm. "You can get comfortable," he said, walking out the door.

"Okay, I will," Felicia said in a warm tone.

Everything about her was smooth, Darnell thought walking down the hall to the bathroom. He got in the shower and lathered up thinking about Felicia and how she would feel. He wasn't going to rush her; he was more than willing to wait because she was worth it. Petie told him the best ones were the ones worth waiting for. Darnell knew what he meant.

CHAPTER TWENTY TWO
VIRGINIA

At headquarters, the agents were getting the necessary paperwork ready to transport Dougie, and his partner, Tony to jail. Dougie whined the whole time while his partner stuck to his guns. They kept them separated. Dougie wondered if his partner had folded like he did. He wondered what he had told them, if anything at all.

One of the agents came to Dougie's cell and through the bars he said, "We're going to talk to the District Attorney and get you out under our custody. You just keep cooperating and everything will be fine."

Dougie jumped off the metal bed with hope in his eyes, and said, "Thank you Sir. Thank you so much. I have a family, wife and a little girl. I can't go to prison, sir."

"Don't worry. We'll get you out of here. Like I said you just keep cooperating with us and everything will be fine, buddy," he said and walked away.

Dougie fell back on the cold metal slab of a bed, turned on his side and cried into his sleeve. The muffled sound could be heard throughout the holding cell area. He did not know that on the other side Tony was listening to him.

He yelled out loud, "You fucken faggot!"

Dougie was processed and housed in Protective Custody unit. He couldn't wait to get to court in hopes that he would be a free man. When he was being shackled along with Tony they had a brief exchange of words. His once close partner had told him, "You better go to P.C. mothafucka!"

Dougie had winced, knowing Tony was wild, and he wasn't taking any chances. He could feel his heartbeat pulsing crazy in his eardrums. They were on opposite sides now so they had nothing in common anymore. Dougie waited until after the count and called his wife. She answered on the fourth ring, sounding half-asleep. "Hello."

"Lisa, it's me," Dougie said after she accepted the collect call. It was the first time he had a chance to call his family.

"Where are you?"

Dougie started crying. "I got in some trouble. They stopped us on the freeway on our way back."

"Oh God," she whimpered. "So where do they have you at now?" she asked, sounding like she was moving around.

"In VA, they said they were going to cut a deal with me so when I see the judge, they're going to let me go. I told them what they wanted to know and they said as long as I cooperate I'm good," Dougie explained slowly.

"Where is Tony?"

"They got him housed in another section. I'm not fucking with him," Dougie said.

"So what are you gonna help them do?" she asked. In the back Dougie could hear the baby crying.

"Whatever they want, all I know is that I'm not doing any prison time and those niggas is still gonna be getting money. I lost $1500 today and all the material. So, whatever they want from me, I'm gonna give it to them," Dougie whispered.

"Oh God, Dougie you can't do that. You know how Petie is. Are you trying to get us all killed?"

"Don't worry about that. I'll let them niggas know that they have to protect my family first before anything," Dougie said, sounding confident.

They talked until chow was called. Lisa took down his information and told him to call her back after he ate. Dougie sat at a table with two other dudes and ate in silence. He dumped his tray and then went back to the phone to call his wife.

In the general population side of the jail, Tony was politicking with the other inmates, telling them what had happened. Inmates who knew the same people Tony knew automatically gravitated to him. They could see his swagger and could tell he was 'bout it. One cat stood over to the side just listening. Tony saw him noting the tattoos on his arm and down his chest. Tony knew him from somewhere but he could not place his face. Something ripe was churning in his stomach as he tried to remember where he knew the dude and his tats. The guy approached Tony slowly and said, "Don't you have a sister named, Stephanie?"

"Yeah, I do why?"

"You don't remember me, dog? I'm Prince."

"Oh yeah," Tony said, giving him a pound.

Prince used to date his sister a few years back for a short time. Tony remembered now that Prince had caught few charges in several states. His sister had visited Prince until he had gotten transferred, and it was too far for her to travel.

"So you were saying that you got caught up on the freeway? How much they took from you?" Prince asked.

"Fifty-grams; those niggas came out of nowhere and rushed us. This crab ass nigga that I was getting money with folded on me.

They put his ass in P.C. when we got here."

"Oh yeah, but even in P.C. we can still get to him," Prince said.

Tony immediately knew that Prince was a 'rat hunter', and just like that, they would get to Dougie.

CHAPTER TWENTY THREE
PENNSYLVANIA

Cliff almost knocked the phone over trying to reach it. He answered it on the third ring.

"Hello," he said sleepily wondering who it was at this hour of the night.

Cliff listened closely feeling the anger and disgust rise in from his gut. It was a phone call he had prayed he would never get. The jail was calling to tell him that Calvin was taken to an outside hospital because he had been sexually assaulted.

"Good God," he said, replacing the receiver on the hook.

He put his head in his hands and wept. Wept because as a father he felt powerless over what his son was going through since this ordeal started. He could not protect his son. He could not give Calvin any comfort and he could not travel this road for him. Cliff felt like he had failed Calvin when he needed him the most to protect him from predators. He quickly got dressed and rushed out the door to go to the hospital where Calvin had been taken. Cliff had to see his son and nobody was going to stop him.

At the hospital, Cliff rushed through the doors and asked a nurse where jail inmates would be treated. He was told to go down to the basement and walk through the double doors and someone down there could assist him. Cliff waited impatiently for the elevator to come then got in it. A correction officer stopped him as he got off, telling him that he was not allowed in the area.

"The hell I'm not! My son was brought to this hospital after being attacked! Now get out of my way!" Cliff shouted.

"Sir, what is your son's name?"

"Calvin Houser."

"He's in with the doctors right now. I'll let you see him when they are finished treating him," the officer said, showing empathy.

"Thank you," Cliff said.

"Have a seat."

"Thank you very much," Cliff said, sitting down. The officer was watching him so Cliff asked, "Can you tell me what happened?"

"He was attacked by several inmates. I must warn you, he's in bad shape. The officer on duty got to him just in time. It could have been worse," the officer explained slowly. "I've seen a lot of attacks in my career, but this here was one of the worse."

"Oh God… Is he going to make it? Tell me," Cliff pleaded.

"Yeah, he'll make it. He's pretty beat up and I'm sure he has some internal injuries. I'll let the doctor fill you in. Just have a seat because it might be awhile," the officer said, walking away.

Cliff waited nearly three hours before he was able to see Calvin. His knees went wobbly when he stepped into the hospital room where his son was unconscious, and handcuffed to the bed. Cliff sat by the bedside, covered his face with his hands and cried.

Calvin's face was badly beaten. He had two broken ribs. His anal cavity was ruptured and torn. The doctor told Cliff that he would heal from the physical wounds but he wasn't sure about the emotional ones. Cliff held his son's hand until he was told that he had to leave. He kissed his son on the forehead and got up slowly. He left the room quietly and asked one of the officers, "What's going to happen next? I mean will he be placed somewhere safe when you take him back?"

"Oh yeah, his housing unit will be changed."

"What about the pricks who did this to him? What's going to happen to them?"

"They will be charged with rape and assault. Listen this happens all the time. Your son was just lucky because a guard caught it before the incident got any worse. She pulled the alarm and that's how we caught the men involved."

"How many...?"

"Five," the officer said.

"I wish I could get my hands on the bastards," Cliff said before getting on the elevator.

He rode up in the elevator, the sight of Calvin lying helpless in that bed replaying in his mind. The tears that dropped from his eyes burned as they rolled down his face. Cliff sat behind the wheel for a while before finally pulling off. It was all Renee's fault. She had to be responsible for what happened to Calvin. Cliff made a U-turn in the middle of the street, heading for her house. He wanted her to know his son was paying for her heroic deed.

The sound of the banging on her door in the middle of the night caused Renee to jump. She went to the window, opened it, looked out, and saw Cliff.

"What the hell is wrong with you?" she asked him.

Donte came in her room seconds later asking, "Mom, who is that?"

"Cliff," she said and stuck her head back out the window.

"Open this fucking door!" Cliff yelled.

"What the hell's wrong with you? Are you out of your mind?" Renee yelled.

Cliff banged and kicked on the door like a madman until Donte swung the door open yelling, "What the fuck is wrong with you are you fucking crazy?"

Cliff tried to barge in but Donte knocked him down. Just as Cliff was hitting the concrete, Renee came down the stairs. He made an attempt to get up but Donte shouldered him back down to the ground.

"Please, don't make me hurt you, Mr. Cliff," Donte politely offered.

"Cliff what is wrong with you? Do you have any idea what time it is?" Renee asked, closing her robe while standing behind Donte.

Cliff put up his hand in a surrendering gesture and got up slowly. Cliff chuckled and then broke down in tears on her doorstep.

"Cliff, what's wrong?" Renee asked, stepping towards him.

Donte moved out of the way and Cliff pushed Renee backwards yelling, "This is your fault!" He was yelling at the top of his lungs and pointing his finger at her. Renee caught her balance after nearly falling over her robe. Donte grabbed Cliff by the collar and shoved him down the steps.

"Get outta here man!" Donte shouted, slamming the door.

"What the heck is wrong with him, mom?" Donte asked, having no idea what had happened. "Mom," Donte said. "What happened?"

Renee paced the floor holding her head. She was crying. A lot was going on in her head and she could not take it. The dam burst like a water balloon. Donte held his mother as she cried on his shoulder. Cliff stood outside yelling and screaming.

"What's he talking 'bout, mom?" Donte asked, trying to comfort her.

Renee pulled away from Donte and stomped to the door. She swung the door open and screamed, "It's not my fault! What the hell do you want from me?"

Cliff quickly raced up the steps, ran to her front door, and grabbed Renee by the throat. He angrily threw her down. But Donte was on top of him before he could blink. Grabbing Cliff by the collar, he hurled the surprised father then head butted him, knocking him backwards. Cliff staggered, falling like a tired boxer who had gone twelve rounds. He rolled over and tried to get up but Donte kicked him in the ribs.

"You trying to hurt my mother...?" Donte yelled.

Renee was on her feet, screaming, and yelling, "Get out of my house before I call the police!"

Donte pulled Cliff up off the floor and pushed him through the opened door. Cliff tripped over his feet, falling down the steps, landing hard on his side. Donte slammed the door shut and locked it. Looking at Renee he asked, "Are you okay, mom?"

"Yeah, I don't know what the hell is wrong with that man. He's lost his damn mind."

"Mom, what happened? Why is he acting like that all of a sudden?"

"He blames me for getting Calvin locked up."

"Locked up?" Donte said incredulously. "When did that happen?"

"Donte, it's a long story," Renee said looking away.

"What did he do something to you, mom?" Donte asked, his concern echoed.

"No, no, no honey, nothing like that. He stole a car and I just happen to witness it. I saw the entire incident, but I did not know that it was Calvin until they had arrested him. I was shocked that it was him," Renee explained. She slowly ran her fingers through her hair then took a deep breath. "Cliff blames me because I called the police and that's why I had to go to court the other day," she said, sighing loudly.

"Ooh," Donte said, eyes widening.

He quickly walked to the window and looked outside.

"Is he gone?" Renee asked.

"Yeah," Donte said, closing the blinds.

"Come on, let's go to bed," Renee said, walking up the steps. "Try that shit again, and you gonna be leaving here in handcuffs," she mumbled to herself.

CHAPTER TWENTY FOUR
NEW YORK

Share sat at Venus' bedside the same way she had been doing every single day since the attack. Her condition had not gotten any better. Share continued her ritual of having a regular conversation with Venus. Share talked about what happened in court. She told Venus how she had called the bank, and spoken with the executives, explaining to them what Andre had done. She laughed remembering the conversation with the executive.

"Are you aware that one of your bank managers has been charged with assault and battery?"

"Who am I speaking with?" the executive had demanded.

"This is the sister of the victim. Andre Daniels beat my sister nearly killing her. He has been arrested and is now fighting a domestic violence case," Share had said slowly, making sure her words sunk in.

The executive had cleared his throat then said, "No we were not aware of that. Mr. Daniels had taken a day off for court but the bank was under the impression that he was fighting a traffic ticket."

"A traffic ticket...?" Share had said incredulously. *"You can't be serious. That monster beat my sister into a coma. She's showing no signs of life. That monster nearly killed her! Now I am a faithful Chase Bank customer, and I would hate for this kind of information to hit the papers. I think you should take some action before I make a call and have every investigative reporter on the bank's steps,"* Share said then waited in silence for a response.

Immediately the executive replied, "Ma'am, the bank does not in any way, shape or form condone any battery on women. And certainly does acknowledge the sensitivity of domestic related attacks. I can assure you that I will turn this information over to the higher ups. That person will look into this and will act accordingly and efficiently, I assure you."

"This is the response I expected. I want to thank you for your time and understanding."

Share continued with telling Venus about the renovations that she was doing at the Fordham restaurant. She wished that Venus would open her eyes, but Share understood it would occur in the Lord's time. She got up and kissed Venus on the forehead. Share headed home and waited for Will.

Will and Derek waited for Kalif at the visiting area. Will walked to the vending machines and got some food for them to eat on the visit. Kalif was sentenced to Manhattan State for his crimes five years ago in the Polo Grounds. He did not serve one day of jail time after being sentenced to a psychiatric center. Testimony at the trial convinced the judge that Kalif was not in his right frame of mind when he had taken Lydia hostage. Kalif was under the influence of PCP and his actions were drug induced. Therefore he was not responsible for his actions on that day, the judge had ruled. The decision outraged the community and the prosecution, but the decision had been upheld. He sentenced Kalif to five years in the psychiatric center. On the visiting floor, Kalif came through the double doors, signed in and went to the table. Like always for the past five years, Derek and Will gave their man a pound and a hug.

"What's good?" Derek asked, sitting down. "You are outta here in what… 38 days my dude?"

"Yeah nigga, I can't wait to hit the streets. Blow an 'L' and get some pussy," Kalif smiled, ear to ear.

He was looking much stockier than when he was arrested. His hair was longer. Kalif still kept it braided only now he had big plaits, not the designer styles he used to wear.

"Speaking of pussy... What's up with that nurse that you were talking about before?" Derek asked.

Kalif had his eyes set on a new nurse that had gotten transferred to his floor.

"Oh, she frontin' talking about her 'job this' and her 'job that'. She knows she wants to give a nigga some pussy," Kalif said, smiling from ear to ear.

Will set some White Castle burgers down on the table and Kalif reached for two of them. Kalif took the burgers out the box and bit into one of them. Derek chewed on a Nathan's frank with mustard and ketchup.

"The next time we come up here will be to pick you up, my dude. The buss is over," Derek said. "Speaking of the bid being over, I hope you're not gonna start smoking that shit again," Will said, sipping out of a Pepsi bottle.

He was looking at Kalif with a thousand watt stare. Kalif felt like his friend was looking right through him. He flashed back to how he began sliding. The thought gave him a chill. It was as if someone had dropped him into a freezer. Kalif took a reassuring breath and said, "Nah, I'm not fuckin' with that shit anymore. Those dust days are over, my dude."

"Good," Will and Derek chorused. They remembered how Kalif used to get when he was dusted, and it was some scary shit.

"So are you still going to take the medication when you leave here?" Derek asked, finishing up his second frank.

Kalif shrugged then said, "I don't know. If I think I need it then I will. But that shit be having me tired and sleepy. All day, all a nigga wanna do is eat and sleep. You see how much weight I put on, right?" Kalif smiled, rubbing his stomach, and patting his chest. "When I get time I drop down and do a couple of sets. If not I would've gotten out of shape. Plus, they have a gym here but these wackos don't be going there, so I get to go myself and get it in," Kalif explained, easing into a bicep flex.

Will changed the subject saying, "We dropped off your clothes when we checked in and we left you twenty dollars in quarters plus a phone card. There's an envelope with 50 singles in it for the machines or in case you wanna buy some pussy from one of these chicks in here." Will laughed at his own joke and said, "I'm only fuckin' with you my dude."

"I know. I'm gonna get all the pussy a nigga needs when I hit the streets. These chicks in here are washed up anyway. The only one worth looking at is walking around making cat noises. The chick must have had a bad experience with a cat or something. I don't know."

They all laughed. The fellas talked and joked around until it was time to leave.

In the car, Will said to Derek, "I really hope this nigga don't smoke again when he comes out. You know people forget how the drugs had them? And they think that they can go back and everything will be different. But it never is... It always picks up where it left off."

"True story," Derek said, pulling out of the parking lot.

ƆHAPTER TWENTY ꟻIVE
ᗺALTIMORE, MARYLAND

Petie sat in his truck behind the wheel, waiting for Tennessee to come out. They were going to Josephine's house to set up shop. She had sold the house to Petie for five-hundred dollars in crack. Petie had the deed to the house transferred to Patrice. They had full ownership of the house, and the property. He wasn't going to fix it up; it was only going to be a safe house.

Taking the back roads, they reached the back of the house in no time. Petie told Josephine that once the deal was done— it was done. Don't come back with a sad story after you broke, and smoked up the material. He warned her.

Petie and Tennessee entered from the back door and walked through the kitchen. The house was nicely structured, but the painting had chipped and the ceiling needed work. Josephine had done like Petie had told her to do and cleaned up the place before she left. He walked through the scarcely furnished house and checked out all the rooms. He went down to the basement, and looked around. When he came back upstairs, Tennessee was in the main bedroom looking through the walk-in closet.

He turned to Petie and said, "Right here I can build another room. It will be small, but it will serve the purpose."

"You can build the room yourself or you want me to get someone to do it?" Petie asked.

"No, I can do it myself," Tennessee answered, turning to face Petie.

Petie shrugged his shoulders and said, "Whatever works. I just want it done. We can go to Home Depot and get the things you need. How long will it take you to get it done?"

"A day and a half, or so… Like I said, it's not going to be a big room. But I'll make sure there's enough space for us to be able to get in and out," Tennessee said, walking out the room with Petie behind him.

"Cool, we'll take a ride over to the shopping center and get the things you need," Petie said as they walked out the back door.

At the shopping center, Petie sat in the truck while Tennessee went inside to get the supplies that he would need. Petie called Chaos to check up on him. Chaos was on his way to Philly to meet with some other dealers that Petie supplied material. When it came down to the business, Chaos always did the traveling. Petie was still a wanted man and kept a low profile. Chaos answered on the second ring.

"What up?"

"How close are you?" Petie asked.

"Another thirty minutes, or so… It's not too much traffic out here. I'll be crossing the bridge soon and I'll holla when I get to Southwest."

"Cool, we went pass Josephine's and took a look around. Tennessee is going to build a room inside the closet. We are at Home Depot now getting what he needs to make it happen. Then we'll work on getting the fencing done," he informed Chaos.

Petie always let Chaos know what he had planned no matter how small. Chaos was his other half like Ladelle had been when he was in New York.

"Is he going to do the fencing too, or are we gonna hire somebody?" Chaos asked.

"I don't know. This nigga seems to be a jack of all spades. So if he can do it then that's even better. I really don't want to mess with no outsiders. I don't want them on the property. I want us to keep this house as low as possible and try getting it off the radar. When the neighbors see the difference, then they will know that it's not a crack house anymore. I was even thinking about getting it painted when I get the fencing done."

"Yeah, I think that would be good," Chaos offered.

"My son can do that. Just do a little something to the outside to give it a different look," Petie added.

Tennessee returned with two shopping carts filled with building supplies. Petie hopped out of the truck and opened the back gate. He told Chaos, "Holla when you get there and let me know what's what."

"No doubt," Chaos said, ending the call.

Petie and Tennessee loaded the items in the back and then made another stop at the hardware store before heading back to the house. He dropped Tennessee off and said, "I'm going to go and pick up some paint so my son can do the outside of the house. I'll check back with you in a few hours."

"I'll be here," Tennessee said.

Once Petie had left Tennessee made a phone call and spoke briefly. He told the person on the other end that he was working, and that things were looking better for him.

"Are you ever coming back?" she asked.

"I can't and you know that," he said, feeling sorry that he could never return to his loved ones.

He could feel the tears building behind his closed eyes. It hurt so much knowing that he may never see them again.

"Stay in touch, baby. We love and miss you so much," she said.

"Me too," Tennessee softly said.

He closed his flip-phone and sat on the edge of the windowsill. Petie had been a blessing to him. He had come into his life at the right time, even though what he was doing was illegal. This gig kept him from begging for money, and not knowing where his next meal was coming from. Tennessee threw himself into the mission he had set out to do. It took his mind off his family he missed so much ever since leaving Ohio.

CHAPTER TWENTY SIX
NEW YORK

Ladelle was leaving Nadirah's house when Bob called him. He had been spending a lot of time with her but still had not taken her to bed. Nadirah had come on to him in so many ways, she turned him off, but Ladelle was still very much attracted to her. He was still married. Even though Lydia had been cheating, Ladelle was not going to do anything that would prevent him from getting sole custody of Ladir. As far as he was concerned, Nadirah was only a friend. He answered the phone immediately when he saw Bob's number.

"What you got for me, man?" Ladelle asked him.

"Photos and more photos- your wife is one busy lady. She seems to have a healthy sexual appetite for her secret lover. She was at the same hotel twice today. She went in the morning after you left, stayed for two hours and then returned after she left the restaurant," Bob informed.

Ladelle felt a familiar tightness in his stomach that he always felt when he thought about Lydia being with another man.

"Do we know who this man is yet?" Ladelle asked.

He wanted to see Lydia's lover, find out everything about him before looking him in the eyes. It would not make a difference because either way the marriage was over. He only wanted Ladir and the restaurant. Anything else she wanted, she could have.

"I didn't find out yet, but I did make contact with one of the maids. And she was a little leery to give out any information. I palmed a fifty in her hand and she said that she would see me tomorrow with the occupant's name of that room," Bob explained, seeming proud of one of the oldest techniques. "Money has a way of persuading people."

"All right, thanks a lot, Bobby. You're the best man. Keep me updated. Where is she now?" Ladelle asked, wondering aloud where his darling, cheating wife was.

"She's at the restaurant in midtown. I have a guy across the street sitting in a mini-van. He is very low key so she'll never spot him. In any event I will call you tomorrow and let you know what happened with the maid."

"All right, Bobby. Let me know the minute you find out and get a description of him while you're at it," Ladelle said, feeling hopeful.

He was one step closer to exposing Lydia, but needed proof. Ladelle pulled up in front of his restaurant and noticed the mini-van. Bobby was right this guy was incognito. Ladelle would never see him and he knew Lydia wouldn't. Ladelle entered the restaurant and went directly to the office. Lydia was behind the desk when he opened the door. She swung around in her chair and smiled warmly at her husband.

"Hey, good looking, what's cooking?"

Ladelle plastered a smile on his face and replied, "Nothing much. You are hot as so I guess you're cooking."

She got up out of the chair, sexy as ever. She sashayed over to where he was standing. Ladelle quickly grabbed her and hugged her kissing her on the neck. He did not know what her lips had been around, and knowing what he did they been around something. He pulled away from her and studied her briefly, wondering if there were stretch marks around her mouth.

"You smell good. Is that a new fragrance you're wearing?" he quickly asked.

The last thing he wanted was her lips touching his. Goodness, those were stretch marks he was seeing.

"No, this is the Giorgio that you bought for my birthday. Don't you recognize the smell?"

"Uh no, I am a little stuffed up," he lied.

"You better go get checked out. Last week you had a cold, and now you're stuffed up," she said with concern.

"Yeah," Ladelle said.

He wanted to ask Lydia was she constipated because she was so full of shit. He could not stand her anymore. At first when Ladelle found out that she was cheating, it hurt. He loved Lydia, but she was turning his love to hate more and more.

"I have to go and see the distributors before they close up. I'll meet you at home," he said and did not wait for a response.

Ladelle left before Lydia had a chance to say anything. His thoughts stirred him and Ladelle made a quick run of the restaurant then he left. He drove to Central Park not far from their luxury apartment, and sat in the car. He started to call Nadirah back, but decided against it. He had plans to see her on Sunday for dinner and a movie.

Andre was chilling in bed watching the porno channel the hotel provided. He called the hospital earlier to inquire about Venus, but was told no information could be given out. He wanted to go and see her but he did not want to run into Share.

Share, that bitch was probably the one who called the bank, and got him suspended. He knew just what Share needed; a real man and not some kid like the one she was involved with. Andre always felt like women who dealt with younger men were insecure and could not handle a real man. That is why they settled for younger men.

Andre stroked himself slowly watching the woman on the television handle two men riding her. One was in the front, and the other was in her back. Slut bucket, Andre thought. Those kinds of women never interested him. Andre had always had good women who catered to him, and came from a good background. Like Jamie, his first wife. The one he had to get rid of. She had started using drugs and in Andre's eyes became dirtier than mud. His erection, once solid enough to break through concrete, slowly dwindled in his hand. His mind drifted to the last night that he had spent with Jamie.

He had just come in from work and he could smell the cabbage on the stove burning. The kitchen was filled with smoke and the detector was ringing angrily. "What the hell," he said out loud, swinging open the kitchen door to get rid of the smoke. Andre stood on the dining room chair, and pulled the battery out of the smoke detector.

"Jamie! Where the hell are you?"

There was no answer. Again he yelled, stomping up the steps, "Jamie! Jamie!"

He heard the toilet flush then water in the sink. Andre turned the doorknob only to find it locked. He banged on the door yelling, "Come out of that bathroom now!"

He knew she was getting high like always. She opened the door slowly, and he pushed it the rest of the way open.

"Get out of here now!" he yelled, pulling her out into the hallway.

She tripped and fell hitting her shoulder against the wall. Her eyes became wide and glassy. Andre turned his head in disgust. She looked terrible. "Get off the floor and get down stairs to the kitchen," he turned around and ordered Jamie.

Her mouth was moving but nothing was coming out of it.

Jamie scrambled to her feet and hurried down the steps. Andre went into the bedroom, and got undressed. He got in the shower with plans to eat what was left of the food that she hadn't burned. He went back down stairs. It was quiet and from where he was standing on the steps he did not see any food on the table, and that made him even more pissed off. Andre slowly descended the steps, and Jamie was on the floor in the corner with a pipe in her mouth. She had the flame on the lighter sky high, sucking the pipe, trying to get all the smoke out of it. Andre lost it. He ran over to her, and smacked the piping hot crack pipe out her mouth. It shattered in pieces, the screen still steaming hot, when the pipe hit the floor.

"That's it! You wanna kill yourself? Okay, well I'll help you!"

CHAPTER TWENTY SEVEN
NEW YORK

Andre jumped up, raced to the bathroom, and splashed cold water on his face. He was sweating like a track runner. He sat in a chair by the window, and tried to think about something else, but his thoughts kept drifting back on Jamie.

He had pulled her up off the floor and smacked her. She fell sideways and hit her head. She had looked up at him through those pancake size eyes and said, "Please don't hurt me. I promise I won't smoke anymore. I promise."

How many times had he heard that? Too many plus Andre knew that this time she was telling the truth because she would not be around to smoke. Andre smiled crookedly at Jamie then said, "I know my dear. Tonight will be your last night smoking." He snatched Jamie up off the floor, and punched her in the face knocking her out cold.

After dragging her into the middle of the floor, Andre got one of the dining room chairs and set it next to her unconscious body. He lifted her off the floor, and sat her in the chair. Her head was tilted to the side, and her hands hung like dead weight by her sides. He looked at her then smirked before hurrying to get the things needed to finish her off. Andre went to the utility closet and got duct- tape, ammonia, bleach and other cleaning supplies. He quickly strapped Jamie to the chair with duct tape. He hurried to the kitchen, and mixed the ammonia, bleach, Ajax and toilet bowl cleaner into a jar. He shook it up until it was foamed. Satisfied with his solution, Andre pulled the other dining room chair in the living room, and sat down.

He slapped Jamie hard one time, causing her eyes to open immediately. She looked at him, not realizing that she was duct taped to the chair, she tried to stand.

"What is wrong with you?" she asked confused and scared at the same time.

"You always said that you wanted to stop getting high and get yourself clean right?" Andre asked.

"Yeah, but…"

Andre cut her off saying, "Well I am going to clean you out now. This is your first day in rehab my dear."

He got up and started squeezing Jamie's jaws together, causing her mouth to open. Andre poured the cleaning solution down Jamie's throat, covering her mouth, and making her swallow it.

Jamie spit and choked trying not to let it go down her throat, but Andre was stronger. After several seconds she was foaming at the mouth and her body shook in convulsions. Andre stepped back and watched her until she fell limp in the chair. He went into the kitchen and filled a pot with cold water and threw it on her. Jamie jumped immediately. She started coughing and gagging until she caught her breath long enough to ask Andre, "Are you nuts?"

"Nuts?" he said. "Now there is an idea."

Andre rushed outside to the porch and picked up a handful of acorn nuts. He rushed back into the kitchen, and started crushing the nuts.

Jamie was screaming, "Help! God somebody help me!"

"Help is on its way!" Andre yelled from in the kitchen.

He added more to what was left in the jar then he put the crushed acorn nuts in and shook it like it was a homemade milk shake. Jamie kicked and screamed while he forced it down her throat. She choked and gagged while Andre held his hand over her mouth.

"Swallow it," he growled, applying pressure to his grip.

He beat Jamie in the head with the pot until she was

unconscious. Andre peeped out the window to make sure that no one heard her cries. It was late. In this small town everyone went to sleep early, it was time for him to really get busy.

Andre went out back and started digging Jamie's grave. It took him several hours but it was finally done. He went back inside to duct tape her mouth and carry her out to her final resting-place. Out of breath and tired, Andre buried Jamie out in the backyard.

He wiped the sweat off of his face and headed back inside the house. That's when he saw her. The elderly neighbor was in her bedroom window looking out from behind sheer curtains. She would have to go too, Andre thought. She spotted him looking at her and quickly got out of the window. Andre jumped over her fence and was at her back door in seconds. He broke the window on the door and was inside her cluttered house.

Andre ran up the steps two at a time, and caught the old woman just as she was reaching for the telephone.

"I don't think you'll need to make that call," he said calmly to her.

Andre was on her in two long strides. He held the pillow over her head tightly until her frail, weak, body stopped moving. Then he propped her up like she was sleeping and pulled the covers up to her neck.

"Good night," he whispered. He quickly left her house and went back to his own.

Andre sat on the couch, sweating and panting. He sat with his head leaned back, thinking, two killings in one night. This neighborhood wasn't safe anymore.

CHAPTER TWENTY EIGHT
PENNSYLVANIA

The count was clear. Calvin lay back on his cot, waiting for the next movement. He had been programmed to the laundry room. The call came over the speakers, announcing a program movement. Calvin exited his cell. He got right in the flow of foot traffic with the other inmates, and went to the huge industry laundry area. The other inmates were already there, pushing baskets of sheets, blankets and towels. He went to the folding section where he worked, and got busy folding the sheets coming out the dryers.

One of the other inmates called Calvin telling him to go to the back and get some detergent from the officer.

"All right," he replied and walked to the back.

Calvin went through the double doors but did not see an officer. Before he could turn around, he was punched in the face. The blow knocked him down on the hard floor, and the impact busted his lip. He looked up, and saw them coming for him. Calvin got up, and tried to fight, but they were much too strong for his slight frame. They dragged him to a corner in the back, shoving towels in his mouth. One after another they raped and beat Calvin, leaving him bloody and bruised. He managed to crawl out to where the other inmates were, and two inmates rushed over to him, rolling him over on his back.

"Get the officer!" one of the inmates, yelled out. Several other inmates crowded around to see what was going on.

"Oh shit! They fucked him up…!" one of them exclaimed.

He shook his head feeling sorry for Calvin. His pants were still down around his ankles, and he was bleeding from his anal cavity.

Blood was leaking out like a faucet and settled in a pool underneath him. The officer on duty pulled the alarm and sat with Calvin until medical arrived.

Calvin woke up and tried to turn on his side but the pain was excruciating. He was back in the hospital again. He did not even remember the ride to the hospital. He had blacked out after the attack. He blinked at the surroundings. Calvin closed his eyes and cried. He could not keep going through this. The attacks had stripped him of his manhood and any dignity that he had.

These scars would never heal and Calvin knew that. The whole jail looked at him like he was some kind of sissy and these inmates were using his body like some kind of dumping waste to relieve themselves. This time it was more of them than the last time. Calvin knew that it would never stop, and he also knew that he could not fight them off. He opened his eyes and wiped away the tears. There was only one way out of this whole situation and he was going to do it now. He would not spend the next umpteen years getting raped repeatedly.

"No more," he said out loud to his self.

He snatched the I.V. out of his arm and went into the bathroom not even noticing the pain. He looked up at the vent then the bathroom floor. It was high enough, he thought as he walked back to the bed. Calvin snatched a sheet off of the bed and ripped it and then ripped another piece, attached it to make it stronger. He went back into the bathroom and prayed before tying the one end around his neck. He took the other end, stood up on the tub, and tied it to the vent in the ceiling. Calvin pulled on it to make sure that it held. Tears were falling down his face like raindrops when he stood on the sink, closed his eyes, and jumped.

Cliff was at his desk when he got the call. He screamed like a wounded animal, he was informed of Calvin's suicide.

"How could you let this happen?" he cried in heart wrenching sobs. "Just tell me how."

"Sir, he was taken to an outside hospital after another brutal attack, and one of the nurses found him in the bathroom."

"No one called to tell me that he had been assaulted again!" Cliff yelled. "Why didn't someone call me? Dammit! I could have saved my son!" he yelled repeatedly.

"Sir, I don't know why you were not notified. I am terribly sorry to have to give you this news. I will personally look into the matter and find out why the staff on duty at the time of the attack did not notify you," the captain said.

"Where is my son's body?"

"He is in the morgue at the hospital…"

Cliff hung up, and rushed out of his office, not waiting to hear what else the prison captain had to say.

CHAPTER TWENTY NINE
BALTIMORE, MARYLAND

Chaos sat in the back and waited. Dougie had called, saying he was coming through, but he was two hours late. He tried to call Dougie back but the phone number he had was not in service.

Chaos called Petie and said, "This nigga didn't get here yet. I don't know if I should close up and bounce or wait for him. What do you think?" "

"How late is he?"

"About two hours. Tennessee is in the back watching the cameras because he said he had a bad feeling. We tried to call him, but the number isn't working."

"Where did he call you from?" Petie asked.

"I don't know."

"You think he got caught up?"

"I don't know," Chaos said, sounding weary.

"I'll be there in a minute," Petie said.

Chaos sat in the back with the dogs at his feet, and waited until finally a car pulled up. The dogs started barking and jumping at the gated fence trying to get out. Chaos stood up; he did not recognize the car but he recognized Dougie behind the wheel. He saw a passenger he didn't know in the car. Dougie got out smiling and said, "We got caught in traffic, fucking accident with three cars. They weren't letting any cars pass."

"Oh yeah," Chaos said, grilling the guy who got out of the passenger seat. "Who the fuck is he?" Chaos asked pointing.

"Oh this is my boy, Black," Dougie said, shifting from one foot to the other.

The guy put out his hand to give Chaos a pound but Chaos ignored him and asked, "Where you from?"

"Washington," Black answered.

Tennessee was in the back watching the cameras and his gut was telling him that something was very wrong. He called Chaos on the cell phone and told him, "Tell that guy to open his jacket."

"Yeah, I am," he replied and closed his phone.

The dogs were barking and growling from deep in their throat, another sign that something was not right. They had seen Dougie a number of times, and they never growled the way they were now.

"Come inside," Chaos said.

He grabbed the dogs by their collars and restrained them enough to let Dougie and Black walk through the gate. Once they were inside Chaos said, "Open your jackets."

Both Dougie and Black did so then closed them back up.

"So where you been, Dougie… and where's your man at? And what's wrong with your phone?" Chaos asked all three questions as if they were one.

"First of all, I lost my phone and I just had it cut off," Dougie said too quickly.

A door slammed outside and the dogs ran out the front door at lightning speed at the same time. Chaos knew it was Petie and did not move.

"So where you been and where your man at?" Chaos asked again.

He sat back and crossed his legs watching the body language between Dougie and Black. Chaos noticed how Dougie had cut his eyes at Black when he asked a second time about Tony. Before Dougie could answer Chaos stood up and pulled out his burner and pointed it at their heads.

"Why the fuck are you so nervous! Open your fucking jackets. Take 'em off and throw them on the floor!" he ordered.

Petie crept in from the side and was watching. He said nothing because he did not have to say anything. Tennessee came in from the side bearing arms, a twelve-gauge shot gun. Chaos looked back and saw Tennessee he said, "Check their fucking pockets before I kill these niggas."

Tennessee went through their pockets only to find a cell phone, a pack of gum and an envelope filled with money. "The pockets are clean," Tennessee said and threw them back on the floor.

"Sit down," Petie said to Dougie and Black. He stared at Black not knowing who he was and then asked him, "Who the fuck is you?"

"Black, I'm from D.C."

"I didn't ask you where you were from. I asked you who the fuck you were," Petie stated, pulling up a chair and sitting across from them. He was holding his meanest dog, Petie by the collar. He looked at Chaos and asked, "How much are they getting?"

"Seventy," Chaos answered not taking his eyes or the nine-millimeter off of them.

"Where's the money at?" Petie asked.

Black answered first pointing to his jacket on the floor saying, "In the envelope in my pocket."

"Get it," Petie said to him.

Black moved slowly, lifting his jacket off the floor, and took the envelope out of his pocket. Black went to pass the envelope to Petie but the dogs jumped at him, nearly taking his wrist off. He dropped the envelope on the floor and jumped back. Chaos picked up the envelope and counted out twenty-one hundred dollars. He passed it to Petie and said, "It's all there."

To Tennessee Petie said, "Give him his shit."

Tennessee went to the back and returned with a large plastic bag filled with raw. He passed it to Dougie but Black reached for it. He took it and asked, "Are you gonna hold the dog when I reach for my jacket?"

Petie still had Petie by the collar and he said, "Go head. You so worried about him, but from what I see he's worried about you."

Black slowly reached down for his jacket and put the raw in the inside pocket. "Can I put my jacket on?"

"Yeah put it on," Petie said. Then to Dougie he said, "Where's Tony at?"

"He ran out on me last week," Dougie lied.

"Oh yeah…?" Petie said. "Shit happens like that when you fuck with the wrong people."

Dougie reached down to get his jacket off the floor when Petie noticed something.

"When did you start wearing glasses?"

"Oh… Um last week…"

"Let me see them," Tennessee said, reaching for the glasses.

He looked at the glasses closely and then tried them on. He walked to the back then came back in a few seconds. He handed the glasses back to Dougie and said, "Where you get them from? Those are a nice set of frames, man."

Dougie scrunched up his face like he was thinking then he said, "You know that eye place that has the fancy commercials."

Tennessee snapped his fingers and said, "Yeah, I know the one you talking about. It's um, Barnes and Noble."

"Yeah that's it!" Dougie replied excitedly.

Black cut his eyes at Dougie and quickly said, "Well if we are all done here, we need to get on the road. We gotta long ride ahead of us."

"Yeah, y'all need to get going," Tennessee said, walking to the back and opening the door.

He watched them get in the car until they pulled off. When he got back inside he said, "Barnes and Nobles...? You know the nigga was lying because that's a book store."

On the road Dougie pulled over at the rest stop with Agent Thomas, a.k.a. Black, and waited for the surveillance units to arrive. Agent Thomas looked at Dougie and said, "I can't believe you fell for that Barnes and Noble's. That was the biggest throw off ever and you fell right into it," he said, shaking his head in disgust.

"You probably just blew everything," he added as he got out of the car when the surveillance vans pulled up alongside them. "Stay here," he said, slamming the car door.

Dougie rested his head on the steering wheel. He had fucked up and he knew it now. Luckily, Tennessee did not notice that the eyeglasses had a microscopic camera attached to the frame. Dougie took off the glasses and checked and the lens was still intact. He could see several agents through the rearview mirror behind the car talking. Some of them laughing, and others were filling out paperwork.

One of them came over and tapped on the window telling Dougie, "You did well. I know it got a little heated at one point, but you handled it well. Good job."

"Thank you, sir. I want to know is my family safe? Can I call them when we get back so that I can make sure?" Dougie asked like a kindergarten would ask his teacher to use the bathroom.

"Yeah, don't worry about that, pal. I'll make sure you get to talk to your family. You can't tell them where you are; just let them know that you are safe and sound."

"Yes, sir," the snitch replied.

Back at the federal agents' safe house where they housed their informants in Virginia, Dougie showered, ate, and called his wife. She answered on the second ring. Dougie could hear music blaring in the background and also the sound of kids playing and squealing like they were in a playground.

"Hello…"

"It's me, baby. I can't talk long, but I want you to know that I am all right."

"Where are you?"

"I'm still in Virginia. They got me in some kind of witness protection program. The judge ordered me released in their custody just like they said it would happen," he told her lowering his voice so they could not hear him.

"So what happens now?" she asked.

"Well, I am going to be working with them. And the judge is going to dismiss my charges. But for now I just want you to know that I am safe. I can't talk too long, but I want you to know that I am alright. Okay Lisa?"

"Oh…okay. I love you," Lisa said.

"I love you too, baby," Dougie said and hung up.

He wanted to be home with his family, but knew he had to do what he had to do first. The agents wanted to build a case against Petie and his team, and were using him to buy material. Dougie knew that he would have to testify in court when it was all done, but he did not care. He was told that they would relocate his family after it was all done, and he would be a free man. He just hoped that that they would relocate his family before Petie got to them.

CHAPTER THIRTY
NEW YORK

"So are you ready to go out in the real world?" the emaciated nurse asked Kalif.

She checked his medication and the prescriptions that the doctor had written for his release.

"Of course I am," Kalif answered with a smirk. "Are you ready for the real world?" he sarcastically asked.

She looked up at him with a frown. Then she called for the doctor to sign out Kalif.

"Please have a seat, the doctor will be here shortly," she said glancing at Kalif's folder.

He walked out to the hallway and sat, waiting anxiously for the doctor. Kalif wanted out. He knew that Derek and Will were outside waiting for him with a freshly rolled blunt. Hopefully it was grape flavored, and not vanilla.

After about thirty minutes the doctor arrived. He signed Kalif out, checked his prescriptions, and the referral the hospital gave him for the outpatient program.

"You're all ready to go, Kalif. Make sure you take your medication as prescribed, and attend the program. If you don't then I guess we'll be seeing you back here again. And we don't want that now, do we?" the doctor smiled.

"No we don't," Kalif said, picking up the envelope with the prescriptions and referral. "Have a good life," he said over his shoulder as he walked to the elevators.

After five long years, Kalif could not get out of the place soon enough. He did not want to spend a second longer. The elevator arrived on the main floor and Kalif stepped lively out onto the polished floor. He could see Will and Derek in the waiting area. Derek saw Kalif before Will did.

"Here he come now," he said To Will.

Will turned around to see Kalif walking with a bounce in his step.

"What's good?" Will said, embracing his second best friend. "You are finally a free man, my dude."

"Yeah, let's get out of here," Kalif said, walking to the exit.

He took one last look back, and breathed deeply. This place had been his home for the last five years, now he was finally free to leave. It was like getting out of prison, and hitting the pavement for the first time. Kalif stopped, looked up at the sun, and smiled. He looked back at his friends. Derek and Will smiled as they watched him. Both had done state time before, so they knew how Kalif was feeling even if he was only coming out of a psyche center.

They got into the car and drove slowly off the grounds. Kalif sat in the passenger seat smiling from the window like a kid. Things had changed in the past five years. Kalif felt like it had been longer. The transition back into the world always seemed that way. He stared at the sky.

Shortly afterwards they pulled up in front of Derek's building. Kalif looked at the people who were standing outside of the corner store. Some of them were new faces to him and a few, he recognized. He got out of the car, and scanned the faces of the guys hanging in front of Derek's building. One of the guys crossed the street smiling.

"What's good? I know you happy to be outta there," he said to Kalif.

"I didn't recognize you, Darryl. What's good, my dude?" Kalif said, leaning in to give Darryl a hug.

Darryl had dreds in his hair now. When Kalif last saw Darryl, he was sporting a Caesar. He had gotten a little taller over the years too.

"Nothin' much; you can see the neighborhood changed a little bit. They trying to fix it up a little sump'n. I got a little girl now, and a set of twin boys," Darryl told Kalif as they walked across the street.

Will went inside the store to get some cigarettes. Derek crossed the street with Kalif and Darryl.

"Oh word?" Kalif replied.

The other faces that he now recognized as they approached the building interrupted him. One at a time they said, "Yo Kalif, what up?"

"When you get out dude?"

"Oh shit…that's Kalif?"

"What it do, my dude?"

Kalif gave each of them a pound answering, "I got out today. Everything is good… You know how I do."

All the fellas stood outside the building talking for nearly an hour. Finally, Derek said, "Let's go upstairs. Stephanie is burning a little something for your home coming."

"Oh yeah, no doubt," Kalif said, rubbing his hands together. "A nigga ain't have a home cooked meal in years." He turned to the crew of guys and said, "I'm gonna holla at y'all later."

Kalif turned and entered the building with Will and Derek. They rode the elevator to the third floor, and walked down to the end of the hall. At the door outside Derek's apartment, the aroma of fried chicken pulled them inside.

Last year, Derek told Kalif he could stay with him and his girl, Stephanie, until he got on his feet. At first Stephanie was against the idea, but Derek explained to her that he and Kalif go back since elementary school, and he was not going to turn his back on him. Reluctantly, she had agreed even though she had told Derek that she had a bad feeling about it. Derek opened the door to their apartment, welcoming Kalif and hoping that Stephanie wasn't right.

CHAPTER THIRTY ONE
NEW YORK

The phone rang three times before Ladelle answered it. He reached for the cordless phone. It was Petie calling.

"Yeah, what's up?" Ladelle asked.

"You my nigga, and you haven't called in about two weeks. What's good?"

"Man, a little bit of everything. I don't even know where to start," Ladelle replied, sounding exasperated.

"What the fuck is it? You got beef?"

"Nah, it's nothing like that," Ladelle answered. He paused then said, "Lydia is cheating. I got pictures of her going in and out of the hotel on 55th Street. She's lying all the time, sneaking out to go meet a man every week, sometimes twice in a week."

"Lydia...?" Petie asked. He was surprised to hear that she was cheating. Then Petie asked, "How long she been creeping on you?"

"Well, long enough for me to know that the courts will grant me full custody of Ladir when it comes to it. I got enough photographs that will prove infidelity, and that she's unfit to be a mother," Ladelle explained.

"Oh shit! Damn, I'm sorry things turned out that way. That's fucked up, La. You know she's going to go after the restaurant and the crib," Petie commented.

"She can have the crib, but I'll fight her to the end for the restaurant. Not over my dead body will I lose my establishment or my son to her," Ladelle said, sitting up in the bed.

"Does she have any dirt on you?"

"Nope; not even a little bit," he said and then thought about Nadirah. To change the subject Ladelle asked, "When is Trice having the baby?"

"Soon, and I can't wait. You know I got everything for my baby girl already. Darnell is doing well; he's working and maintaining like I knew he would when he got out here. Everything is everything with me," Petie said.

They talked for nearly an hour before hanging up. Ladelle checked the time on the clock. It was almost time for him to pick Ladir up from school. He called the restaurant to speak with Lydia but she was not there. He then called Bob to find out where she was. The private detective and personal friend answered immediately. He informed Ladelle that Lydia was at the hotel again. He had a room number and he would soon find out who occupied the room where Lydia went for her frequent rendezvous.

"That's good to hear. See if you can get a picture of him. I need everything I can get before I file for divorce," Ladelle said, picking up his keys off the coffee table.

"Got you, brother, just give me some time. I'll get everything I can get for you. I am sitting outside of the hotel now waiting for her to leave. As soon as she does I'll let you know."

"All right," Ladelle said, heading out the door.

He was on his way to pick up Ladir. He locked up his front door before getting on the elevator. Ladelle felt sad, but at the same time he was relieved that at least he knew all the facts. Some husbands never know what hit them.

After taking a quick shower, Lydia got dressed faster than a platoon in boot camp. She combed her hair and touched up her make-up like she was a stylist on a movie set. She wanted to be back at the restaurant by now, but her lover had taken his sweet time. She hated when he did that. He knew she only had time for quickies-nothing else. No romancing no foreplay, just get it in and run. He reclined on the bed watching her getting dressed, and doing her make-up. He started to get up, mess up her hair, and pull her skirt over her head just for the hell of it.

"When will I see you again?" he asked.

"Tomorrow evening if I can get away," she said, reaching for her pocketbook on the nightstand.

He got up and snatched her pocketbook out of her hand then threw it on the floor. He thrust his tongue in her mouth, and held the back of her head to him while his tongue forced its way in. He continued holding her until she bit down on his tongue, causing him to pull away. He pushed Lydia on the bed and grabbed at her blouse. The first three buttons popped off and landed on the carpet.

"What is wrong with you, boy?" she asked, reaching down for her buttons.

"What do you think, that you're just going to come and get your rocks off and leave? How long do you think I'm gonna let you get away with that?" he asked her with a cold tone.

Lydia ignored him. She walked around to the other side of the bed, and picked up her pocketbook. Her cosmetic case, comb, and a few hairpins had fallen out on the carpet. She picked them up scowling and pissed off. She looked back at her lover, and rolled her eyes.

He laughed at her and stood in the corner watching her collect her things. Lydia shouted, "You popped the buttons on my blouse! How the hell am I suppose to go outside like this?' She glared at him and then stomped out of the room.

He went into the bathroom and turned on the shower. He was laughing quietly to himself. He loved to see Lydia mad and upset.

She was extra sexy when she was mad. She had so much fire in her eyes, and it turned him on tremendously. He walked around to the closet to get a towel out. He saw it. Something silver like aluminum foil. He bent down and picked it up. It was aluminum foil he thought, walking over to the nightstand. He set it down and then carefully opened it. The white powder inside shimmered like diamonds. He put his pinkie finger on the powder and then to his lips. The taste was so strong that it numbed his tongue immediately. Pure fish scale.

"Well, well, well," he said out loud.

He closed the foil back up and then flushed it down the toilet. He got in the steaming shower and to his self he said, "All this time I thought you had so much energy because you were a Power Puff girl, only to find out that you're a powder puff girl."

CHAPTER THIRTY TWO
PENNSYLVANIA

Renee spotted Cliff's car parked outside as soon as she turned the corner. She was not in the mood for his dumb shit at all. She parked and the minute she turned off the car, Cliff got out of his car, walking toward her. Renee turned off the engine and calmly said, "Cliff what is it?"

"You killed him!" he yelled.

"What the hell are you talking about!" she yelled back at him.

She swung open her car door. Renee had enough of his theatrics. He grabbed Renee by the throat and started choking her while yelling, "You killed him! You killed him!"

All the yelling attracted Donte who was in the house studying. He came running out of the house like a linebacker and tackled Cliff; holding him down by the throat. Cliff struggled to get up, but he was no match for Donte.

Renee rubbed her now bruised throat, and kicked at Cliff as he was on the ground. She shouted while kicking him, "Are you crazy! Huh? You sick son of a bitch! Are you out of your mind?" She kicked at his face, his mid-section and his back frantically all the while yelling, "It's not my fault dammit! Whatever you are talking about it's not my fault!"

Cliff covered his face to keep from being kicked there because Renee's heels had already cut him on his forehead. She kept on kicking him until she started crying in heaving sobs.

"It's not my fault," she cried emotionally.

Donte moved to comfort his crying mother. Her body shook

as she wept in heart wrenching sobs. Cliff got to his feet and pointed at Renee telling her, "My son hung his self in a hospital room. They raped him repeatedly until he could not take it anymore. Did you know that? They raped my son," he said slowly making sure that Renee understood.

She looked up at him with tear-stained face and said, "Cliff, I am so sorry, but you have to stop blaming me. It is not my fault. I'm sorry that I was there that morning. I am sorry what happened to Calvin, hell I wish I were never there that morning, but as fate has it I was."

Renee stared at Cliff hoping that what she had said sank in. He stared at her with an unreadable expression. He had a blank look in his eyes. Cliff turned and walked back to his car. He got in and before pulling off he glared at Renee with a look of disgust and hatred.

Later that evening Donte was studying when the phone rang. He checked the caller I.D. before answering the incoming call from Baltimore. Donte was anxious to speak to his father.

"Hey dad, what's up?"

"It's Darnell. Where's mommy at?"

Donte had not spoken to his brother since he had left to go down south. He missed Darnell but he still had not forgiven him for what he had done to Sonya. Plus, the house had been more peaceful since Darnell left. There was so much he wanted to say to Darnell but did not know where to start.

"She is lying down. She and Cliff are arguing because of something that had happened with his son and he's blaming Mommy.

She's stressed out, crying and worrying about if he's gonna try to hurt her again," Donte informed his older brother.

"Hurt her again?" Darnell exclaimed. "What the hell did he do to her?" he asked.

"He was choking her. Last week he attacked her, and I had to wrestle him to the ground. I was gonna call dad, and tell him, but mom said not to. She said she could handle it."

"Is she hurt?" Darnell asked with concern.

"Nah, her neck is bruised, but she's mainly sad behind it all. She's not scared. You know mommy be fighting. She was kicking him in his face and everything. He was bleeding from his forehead when he got up off the ground," Donte told Darnell.

"Oh word?" Darnell said.

He never liked Cliff anyway. Darnell always felt his mother should not be with anyone else other than Petie.

"Yeah, I held him down for her," Donte said. And then to change the subject he asked his older brother, "How you been? Everything's good out there?"

"Yeah, I'm doing construction work from six in the morning until two in the afternoon. I like it out here. Dad is gonna help me get a car in a few weeks. I'm doing well," Darnell said proudly.

"I'm happy to hear that," Donte said sincerely.

He loved his older brother to death, and had always worshipped the ground Darnell walked on. They were both silent on the phone until Darnell said, "Yo, Donte… I…uh… You know I'm sorry about that. I don't know what I was thinking about that day. I wasn't trying to hurt her. I just… Well you know, I'm sorry for what I did."

"Thank you Darnell. That's all I wanted for you to do was say that you was wrong, and that you were sorry. That was messed up what you did and I appreciate you saying that."

"Yeah no doubt, for what it's worth let Sonya know that I'm sorry for that shit too. Tell her that... You know that I apologize. Plus, I got somebody in my life that I really like and if someone did that to her, I'd kill them on the spot. So I know now how you felt that day, Donte..."

"That's good to hear, and I'm glad you understand and you apologize. So when are you coming back out to visit and tell me about your friend?"

"I don't know. I work Monday through Friday, and I spend the weekends with my friend. She's a senior in high school, only child, and she's a mommy's girl. She doesn't drink or smoke weed. She just studies and goes to school. Her mom lets her come over on the weekends, but she gotta be home before it gets dark. I really like her. She's someone I would marry if it came to that. Daddy likes her and so does Patrice."

"That's all good, Darnell. I'm happy for you. Make sure you send some pictures for me and mommy," Donte said.

"I will. Tell mommy I said I love her, and I'll call tomorrow," Darnell said before hanging up.

Donte hung the phone up feeling a little better knowing that his older brother was changing. He loved Darnell so much and he wanted the best for him like he wanted the best for himself. Donte got up and walked up the steps to his mother's room to tell her that Darnell had called. The door was cracked and he could see Renee on her knees praying. Now was not the time to disturb her, he never disturbed her when she was praying. Donte quietly walked back down the stairs, and back into the living room.

He focused and went back to studying, thinking about the phone call with Darnell. He knew that Darnell was going to tell Petie. Once their father knew everything then the preacher would be praying

CHAPTER THIRTY THREE
BALTIMORE, MARYLAND

Darnell hung up the phone, and called Felicia. She was not home yet so her mother said, "I'll tell her to call you when she comes in, Darnell."

"Thank you, ma'am," Darnell politely said, and hung up.

He went to the basement where Petie was shooting pool. Petie looked up from his one-man game and said, "What's good?"

Darnell leaned against the wall and replied, "Mom was fighting."

He knew that was all he had to say to get his father's undivided attention. Petie set the stick down and said, "What? Fighting who?"

Darnell pushed off the wall and answered, "Her friend, that guy she's been seeing, Cliff. Donte said Cliff spazzed on mom and started choking her. Donte said that mom was kicking him in the face while he was holding Cliff down. They jumped him outside the house."

Darnell laughed at the mental picture. The idea of Renee and Donte jumping Cliff was really funny to him.

"What are you laughing at?" Petie asked.

"I just can't see mommy fighting."

"What? You just don't know. Your mother will get it in. When we were younger she stayed fighting. She was putting the beats on chicks left and right," Petie said smiling, remembering how Renee used to be quick to fight.

"Are you serious, dad?"

"Am I? Your mother was laying chicks out with the quickness," he said, picking up the phone to call Renee.

The idea of some nigga putting their hands on Renee still had him feeling some kind of way. He wanted to speak to Renee, and hear her side of this story. He wanted to know she was okay.

"Dad, don't tell her I told you because Donte said that she did not want to call you. She told Donte that she could handle it." Darnell said.

Petie put the phone down and said, "All right I'll call her later and see what's what." He picked up his pool stick and to Darnell he said, "Let's play a round before I get out of here."

Darnell picked up the other pool stick and shot pool with his father for nearly two hours. Then the telephone rang. Petie let it ring until after he set up his shot. It was Chaos calling. Petie reached for the phone on the wall near by the door. "What up?"

"You need to come over. We gotta talk," Chaos said sternly.

"Oh yeah," Petie replied.

He knew that when something was important Chaos would not discuss it on the phone and he could tell by Chaos' tone that this was very pressing.

"I'm on my way now," Petie said and hung up. To Darnell he said, "Brush up on your game until I get back."

He ran up the stairs two at a time and out the backyard where he was parked in the driveway.

At the spot, Petie knew that it was serious when he saw Chaos pacing. Tennessee sat with a stern face. He pulled up one of the chairs and sat down in it. His dog Petie was at his feet the minute he sat down.

"Talk to me," Petie said, looking at Chaos then Tennessee.

His gut was tight like a knotted string, and that was definitely not a good sign. Chaos stopped pacing and said, "This nigga Tony that used to come here with Dougie, called some people telling them that that Dougie was working with the under covers." He stopped and rubbed his forehead before saying, "The cat he called, called some girl, and the girl called Sissy telling her. She knew that Sissy rocks with us. So she hollered at her the minute she got the call."

He stopped and stared at Petie's facial expression. Petie stood and calmly said, "Get everything out of here. Don't leave anything, not even fingerprints behind."

Tennessee was already headed to the back. Chaos started packing up all the guns and armor that they had in case of gunplay. Petie went out back and looked around for signs of anything strange or out of the ordinary. He pulled out his cellphone and called one of his connects. The person answered on the first ring.

"What up, Petie?"

"I need Dougie's address," Petie said. "Get it to me as soon as you can."

"I'll call you back in an hour," the person said and hung up.

Petie walked around to the side of the house and looked down the block. No cars were out of place. Everything looked like it normally did. Chaos and Tennessee came out with garbage bags filled with material, guns and paraphernalia. In the back of an old pick-up truck, Chaos put everything in and closed the doors. Tennessee got behind the wheel and headed to the house that they had taken from Josephine.

"I'll be back," he said out the window.

He pulled off and the tires kicked up gravel as he turned out the back road. Chaos turned to Petie and asked, "Should we torch it?" He looked at their safe house that was no longer safe.

"Nah, it'll cause too much attention," Petie said, opening the back door to his Denali, and letting the dogs jump in one by one. "Meet me at the other house," Petie said before he got in the driver's seat.

Petie pulled off and headed to Josephine's old house that was now his. Tennessee had built the private room in the back of the closet and the fencing was done. This house was better than the other place, and it would serve its purpose until Petie could find another location.

Chaos did one last check to make sure that they had not forgotten anything before he left in his car. Every now and then Chaos would pull over, or make an unnecessary turn to make sure that he was not being followed. When Chaos was sure that he wasn't being tailed then he headed straight there.

His palms were sweaty, a clear sign he was worried. Petie's truck was parked across the street. The dogs were running around the front yard, becoming familiar with the place. Chaos parked and crossed the street while keeping an eye out for any cars that seemed out of place in the neighborhood. Petie was inside the house talking to someone on his cell phone. He turned and looked at Chaos briefly and then took a pen out of his inside pocket. Not having anything to write on, Petie wrote on the wall. Chaos looked over Petie's shoulder to see what he had written. It was an unfamiliar address in South Carolina. He figured it had something to do with Dougie.

Petie said into the phone, "Yeah, I appreciate it." He closed his phone and to Chaos he said, "We gonna take a trip tonight." He walked pass Chaos and outside to his truck. Over his shoulder, Petie said, "I'll see you in a few hours."

"Alright," Chaos called out to him before closing the door.

CHAPTER THIRTY FOUR
NEW YORK

Ladelle turned the corner at Nadirah's house, and slowly drove down her block. There were kids playing in the street. He was just about to park when he noticed Lydia's car. It was parked in the circular driveway of Nadirah's Riverdale upscale house. Ladelle drove pass the house, made a U-turn, and circled back just to be sure it was Lydia's car. He did not slow down because he was sure that it was hers by the sticker that he had placed on her bumper.

"What the hell?" he said out loud as he turned off of her block.

Ladelle drove down two blocks and then pulled over and parked. He called Bobby to find how long Lydia had been going to Nadirah's house. He had never seen any pictures of her and Nadirah together and he had never even seen them have any conversation at the restaurant. How long had they known each other?

Bobby answered on the fourth ring. "Yeah," he said sounding out of breath.

"Bobby, its Ladelle. Um, I was wondering who have you got watching Lydia today?" Ladelle could hear moving around and then papers being shuffled.

"I got Adam on her tail today. He's an excellent investigator. Why do you ask?"

"Could you contact him and ask him where she is at?

"Yeah, I could give him a call. Is everything all right?"

Ladelle could hear confusion in Bobby's voice, but he was not going to tell him that his wife was parked outside Nadirah's house. Instead he said, "I called her and she did not answer so I was just wondering what she was up to."

"Lemme give you a call back. I'll call Adam and find out where she is," Bobby said and laughed. "I'll call you back."

Ladelle clicked off his cellphone and set it on the passenger's seat. He leaned his head back on the headrest and waited. What the hell was Lydia doing at Nadirah's? Were they trying to set him up? Did Lydia know that Ladelle had been to Nadirah's house a few times?

"Goddammit!" he said, banging his hand on the steering wheel in frustration.

If Lydia knew that he had spent time with Nadirah then he could not divorce Lydia and accuse her of infidelity, he was guilty too. He banged his hand harder on the steering wheel. What were they up to? Unanswered questions raced through Ladelle's mind. He could feel a headache threatening to come just from the bewilderment that he was feeling. His cellphone rang. Ladelle anxiously picked it up knowing it was Bobby.

"Hello..."

"Adam says she's in Riverdale. He says she's been there for almost an hour. He has pictures of a woman answering the door right before Lydia went inside. Shortly afterwards a man arrived by cab and the three of them have been inside ever since."

"Riverdale...?" Ladelle asked like he did not know. "How many times has she been there?"

"That was the next thing I was going to tell you," Bobby said. "He says to his knowledge she has never been there. This is a new location that we don't have any record on. Obviously she has a new friend."

"Yeah, let me know when she leaves," Ladelle said, clicking off.

He pulled out of the parking spot recklessly, and headed

back to Manhattan.

Kalif walked down 125th Street, taking notice of all the new stores, and old stores. Shit had changed in the past five years since he had been away. He thought, shopping before strutting to 116th Street to see what was up with this female he used to deal with. Not knowing if she was still living there or not, Kalif rang the intercom first, then knocked on the door.

"Who is it?' A woman's voice with static came through the intercom.

"Kalif, is Tina home?"

"No, she's at work."

"Could you tell her Kalif stopped by?"

The door buzzed open, Kalif hurried and pulled the door open before it stopped buzzing. He took the stairs to the third floor and knocked on Tina's door. A woman that Kalif assumed was her mother opened the door.

"Can I leave you my number, and you give it to Tina?" Kalif said.

"Yeah, hold on," she said, disappearing into the apartment. She returned with a pen and pad. "Write it down," she said giving it to Kalif.

He leaned against the wall and wrote down his cell number from the phone that Will had given him.

"Here you go, ma'am. Thank you."

Before he could turn around Tina's mother said, "I hope you ain't a drug dealer. Tina done changed her life around. She ain't running the streets no more. And I don't want her dealing with no dope dealers."

"No ma'am, I'm no dealer or thug. I'm just trying to live right, and do right, that's all," Kalif said.

Kalif noticed she was dead serious. He was happy to hear that Tina had changed because the Tina that he remembered was terrible.

"All right then I'll tell her to call you," her mother said and closed the door.

Outside Kalif walked down 116th Street. He was about to get in a cab but he decided to stop and get something to eat. He crossed the street and went into a restaurant that was also new to him.

Ladir's Soul Food Restaurant, the awning read. He went inside and walked through the double doors. At the take-out center, he had a seat and looked at one of the menus. The food wasn't that expensive, but it wasn't cheap either. Kalif waited for the woman behind the counter to approach then he ordered.

"I'll have the beef ribs, yellow rice, and a side of collard greens," he said, passing the menu back to her.

She set it in a pile over to the side, and wrote down his order before giving it to the cooks. Kalif turned around in his seat and observed the dining area. His eyes were set on a pretty waitress when he saw him. Kalif wasn't sure. He focused closely on the man who was walking around and talking with people at their tables. He remembered his name like he knew his own. Ladelle continued to browse the tables and make small talk with diners.

Because of him and Petie, Kalif's brother was dead. It was because of them that he spent five years in a mental institution. All the beef five years ago triggered nothing but havoc. Kalif felt his chest filling with anger, and his stomach tightening. He stared at Ladelle with a watchful eye until the waitress set his food in front of him. Kalif looked at the plate and said, "This is to go." He turned back around in his seat, watching Ladelle like a hawk. She put his food in a carry out carton and bagged it.

"Here you go," she said with a friendly smile.

"Who is that guy?" Kalif turned to her and asked.

"Oh that's the owner, Ladelle," she glanced and said.

"Ladelle...?" Kalif repeated then he picked up his bag to leave.

"Sir, you forgot to pay!" the waitress called out.

He stopped, went into his pocket, and threw twenty dollars on the counter. Then Kalif walked out, stopped a cab in the middle of the block, and quickly got in. He rattled off Derek's address where he was staying until he got his own place. Kalif could not get Ladelle's image out of his mind. Ladelle was acting like a big shot, prancing around his restaurant with a phat smile on his face.

He got out of the cab and crossed the street. In the lobby, a few of his peeps were shooting dice and blowing trees.

"What up, Kalif?" one of them said and gave him a pound as they bumped chests.

"Ain't nuthin," Kalif said, pushing the elevator button.

His forehead and hands were sweaty as he got on. Seeing Ladelle created a lot of emotions in him. Kalif thought Ladelle had disappeared like Petie. He wondered if Will and Derek knew that Ladelle was still in Harlem. Maybe they just did not bother to mention it. He walked in the apartment and his cellphone rang. He looked at the number with no name.

"Who is this?"

"Tina, how are you doing Kalif? My mom told me that you had stopped by. When did you come home?" she asked in one breath.

"Oh I came home last week..." Kalif said, sitting on the couch.

CHAPTER THIRTY FIVE
SOUTH CAROLINA
CHARLESTON INTERNATIONAL AIRPORT

The terminals were crowded when Petie and Chaos got off the plane. They moved purposefully, heading to the locker area. Petie's contact had rented a locker, and in it contained two weapons, gloves, directions to Dougie's family's house, and a set of car keys to an old, untraceable Oldsmobile.

In the parking lot, Petie called his contact to find out if anything had changed. His contact said, "Everyone is in the house. I drove by there about fifteen minutes ago. All systems are going my man."

Thirty minutes later, Petie and Chaos pulled up in front of the two story brick house, and parked across the street. They decided that it was time to get busy after watching the house for several minutes. Petie started the car, and drove two blocks away. They parked and headed back to their destination.

The house was in darkness with the exception of an upstairs bedroom light. Chaos put on his black leather gloves and rang the doorbell. Inside the house they could hear the bells chiming three times. Petie stood on the side of the house, keeping his hand on the chrome in his pocket.

"Ring it again," Petie said to Chaos.

Chaos rang the bell again and pulled the skullie down over his eyes. Moments later from inside the house they could hear footsteps approaching the door and then the click of the peephole being moved to the side.

"Yes, who is it?" a woman asked.

"It's Jonathan. Dougie asked me to come by and drop some

money off to Lisa," Chaos said disguising his voice.

"Oh, okay hold on," she said.

Seconds later the door opened. Chaos pushed her down, and stepped inside while Petie closed the door behind them. Out of nowhere a Rottweiler came charging out of the kitchen. Chaos shot the dog twice with his silenced weapon and stepped over the lady and the dead dog. Petie looked down into the woman's eyes and saw nothing but fear. She was holding her hand over her mouth, and crying. He stared at her for a few seconds then asked quietly, "Who are you?"

The terrified woman replied, "Dougie's mother, please don't hurt us. We did not know what he was doing." She muffled her cries in her hand.

Petie said, "I know you didn't. I don't think he knew what he was doing either."

He shot her twice in the chest and walked toward the staircase. Chaos was looking at family pictures that were mounted on the walls and in the china cabinet.

"Nice looking dead family aren't they," he said to Petie with a weird look on his face.

They quietly walked up the steps, and listened at the closed doors of each bedroom. In one of the rooms a woman's soft moans could be heard coming through the door.

"Somebody's getting their back dug out," Chaos observed.

Petie hit him with a blank stare. Sometimes Chaos' remarks were out of place when there was work to be done. Petie turned the knob slowly with his gloved hand and pushed the door open to a crack. There was a woman on all fours with a big, burly man behind her. He was getting busy spreading her cheeks and ramming his dick deep inside her dripping pussy.

Chaos walked up behind the guy and hit him with the butt

of the gun. The guy fell over and grabbed at the back of his head leaking blood. The woman started screaming and pulling the cover over her naked body.

"What the fuck!" the man yelled with venom.

He went to move, but not quickly enough. Petie shot him in mid-stride. Then he kicked him back to the floor before shooting him twice in the head. Chaos jumped on the bed, and stood over the woman smirking.

"Who are you?"

She stuttered and covered her face into the pillow. Chaos snatched the pillow from her violently and asked again, "Who the hell are you?"

Petie stared at the woman with contempt. He knew who she was. Petie had seen a picture of her in a pendant on a chain Dougie wore around his neck.

She stuttered with fear and said, "Li-Lisa."

"Dougie's wife...?" Chaos asked.

He made it sound like he was telling her. She slowly nodded.

"So then you know why we are here? Your husband's a rat who doesn't give a fuck about y'all. Now he has cost y'all to pay with your lives."

Without another word Chaos shot her once in the head and a second time in the chest. The impact from the .44 magnum threw Lisa's body back off the bed. Her head tilted off to the side in an awkward way when she hit the floor.

Both Chaos and Petie silently headed to the other two bedrooms. Petie did not know who else was in the house. He moved quickly. From what he had been told only family members were there, but they could not take any chances.

Chaos who was always pumped up after a killing said, "I'll take this room and you get the other one. We need to be outta here."

Petie nodded his head and walked down the carpeted hallway to the last room. He pushed open the door and walked over to the two twin sized beds. In one of them was a young female an in the other was a young male. Petie killed them both as they slept. He then turned and walked out of the room, closing the door behind him. He could hear talking coming from the other room so Petie went in that direction.

Chaos was standing over the queen size bed with the gun pointed at a couple who were in the bed.

"I...I swear we didn't know what Dougie was doing," the woman said, looking at the man who was in the bed with her.

The man added, "We don't snitch on people. We'll forget that you were even here… Please don't hurt us."

He grabbed a hold of the woman as she wept in his arms. Chaos looked back at Petie and smirked. Then he informed him, "This is Dougie's niece and her man. They say they won't tell on us," Chaos said mocking the man.

"I know they won't tell, and don't worry, this won't hurt," Petie said and shot the boyfriend in the center of his eyes.

The niece screamed and Chaos shot her in the face. The bullet tore her face apart leaving only half of her head. They turned to leave and in the doorway was a little boy rubbing his eyes in his Spider Man pajamas.

He looked at them and said softly, "I want mommy."

Petie bent down in front of him and picked him to carry him out the room. How had he missed him when he had gone into the other bedroom? Chaos was right behind Petie when he set the boy down.

"Where the fuck did he come from?" Chaos asked, looking down at the toddler.

"I don't know where shorty was at," Petie replied, staring at the little boy.

He turned to Chaos and said, "Make sure we didn't miss anyone else. Check the attic and I'll go down to the basement."

"Ahight," Chaos said, walking to the steps that lead to the attic.

Petie told the little boy to sit on the floor until he came back.

"I want mommy," the toddler whined on the verge of tears.

"Yeah, I know. Just be a good little boy and wait here," Petie said and went down the steps to the basement. Moments later he returned, Chaos was standing on the second floor looking down at the infant.

"Let's get out of here," Petie said.

"What about him?" Chaos asked, motioning to the boy.

"What about him? Let's go," Petie said heading to the back door.

Chaos continued to stare at the boy until he heard a door open downstairs then Petie called out, "Let's go my nigga!"

Chaos quickly carried the boy into the bedroom and sat him on the bed. Without thinking twice, he shot the infant in the temple. He rushed down the steps, racing to the car.

When they were both inside the car Petie asked, "What the fuck took you so long?"

Chaos positioned himself behind the wheel and started the car. He said nothing until they were on the expressway. "I had to put that kid to bed," he said, cutting his eyes at Petie. He refocused on the traffic. Petie knew what time it was.

CHAPTER THIRTY SIX
NEW YORK

Ladelle looked at the pictures of the man that Lydia had been having the affair with. He was tall, impressive and very handsome. Bobby sat in the passenger's seat, passing him more pictures of Lydia's secret lover. Until a disgusted but relieved, Ladelle had a face to put to the mystery.

Ladelle had seen him before at the restaurant having dinner with a woman, and then he had been there a few times by himself. The restaurant was where Lydia had met him, and started having the affair. As if reading Ladelle's mind Bobby asked, "So do you know him?"

"I've seen him at the restaurant a few times, but that's all," Ladelle replied dryly. "I never had a conversation with him if that's what you mean," he said, putting the pictures in the glove compartment. "Is this the same man that was at the Riverdale house last week?" asked Bobby.

"I'll guess that it is but I have not gotten the pictures back yet. I'll have them tomorrow for you," Bobby said, patting Ladelle on the back. "Rest assured, I will have everything you need by the time you file for divorce."

"I know you will," Ladelle said weakly.

He waited until Bobby left then he called Lydia. He wanted to tell her that he knew everything, and that she was going down. He wanted to tell her that she was a liar and an unfit mother. He wanted to tell her that she should just pack her shit, and leave now before it got ugly, instead he said, "Hey, babe is everything alright?"

"Yeah, everything is fine baby. What time are you coming

in?"

"I'm on my way now. I'll see you shortly."

"Okay, I'll be waiting," she said, sounding sexy before she hung up.

Ladelle checked his watch then started his car. He drove home slowly thinking about his cheating wife who he loved so much.

Kalif went into the store. He brought a grape flavored blunt, a pack of cigarettes, and a pack of condoms. He was anxious about seeing Tina tonight. Kalif was picking her up from work, and they were going to a hotel. This would be his first time with a woman in five years. Kalif was going to tear that pussy up. Every time he thought about Tina, his dick would get harder.

After speaking to her for the first time last week, they decided they would get together tonight. Tina had told Kalif that tonight would be perfect. She would be off from work and could stay overnight with him. She really had changed a lot, Kalif thought as he rolled his blunt. Tina told him that she had stopped drinking and smoking. She was high on life and doing the right thing.

Kalif didn't give a damn about Tina's new and improved lifestyle. Whatever, he just wanted some coming-home-ass. Good for you, ma. Now spread your legs. Kalif sat in the living room, smoking the blunt, waiting for Tina's call.

He checked the clock on the kitchen wall, noting in another thirty minutes or so she would be off. Kalif smoked slowly, thinking that the only thing missing from his blunt was a little dust. That would set everything off right. He inhaled slowly, enjoying the taste of the weed. Stephanie came out of the bedroom and walked into the kitchen.

"I didn't even know you were home Steph. What up?"

"Nothin' I'm waiting for Derek to come home. We're going over to my mother's for dinner," she replied without looking at Kalif.

"Oh okay, well have a good time," Kalif said as she walked past him and back into her bedroom.

She slammed the door and the music was blasting. He knew that Stephanie didn't like him, but he gave her respect, and was always polite. His phone rang, and Kalif anxiously pulled it out of his pocket. It was Tina calling telling him that she was leaving work.

"Good, so we'll meet at the hotel on 145th Street and Amsterdam," Kalif said, getting off the couch and putting the condoms in his pocket.

"Alright, I'll be there," Tina said before hanging up.

Kalif strutted out the door with the lyrics of B.I.G. on his tongue *"I'm fuckin' you tonight..."*

CHAPTER THIRTY SEVEN
PENNSYLVANIA

Cliff left the burial ground where he had just laid his son, Calvin to rest. He sat in his car for a while before sadly pulling out of the cemetery. Everyone else had already left. Cliff had to tear himself away from his youngest son's resting place.

At the end of the winding road, leading out of the cemetery, Cliff sat in his car thinking what had to be done. He turned out of the parking lot and rushed home. The sun was just setting as he made his way back outside. In his car he called Renee hoping that she would be home. The phone rang several times before she answered.

"Hello…"

"It's me Cliff… I was wondering if I could come over and talk to you."

"Talk about what, Cliff?" Renee asked, clearly annoyed by the sound of his voice.

"I just want to see you, Renee. Can I come over and see you?" he pleaded.

"No, I don't think that would be a good idea. You came here and attacked me, threw me on the ground, and choked me. Now you want to talk? I don't think so, Cliff. Take care of yourself and for whatever its worth, I am truly sorry about Calvin. Goodbye Cliff," Renee said slowly, making sure that he understood her every word before she hung up.

Cliff looked at the screen on his phone displaying 'call ended'. She had really hung up on him and he could not believe it. Oh freakin' well, he thought pulling off, and heading to Renee's house.

Renee finished washing the dishes that she and Donte had used for dinner when the doorbell chimed. From upstairs Donte shouted, "Mom, do you want me to get it?"

Renee dried her hands on a kitchen towel and said, "No I'll get it."

She hung the towel back up and walked into the living room where she looked outside through the blinds. Renee took a deep breath then through the door she asked Cliff, "What do you want?"

"I just want to talk to you, Renee. Please open the door."

"Cliff we have nothing to discuss. Now please leave; get off of my property."

"Renee we have to talk," Cliff said, his voice rising a little.

"I said get off of my property," Renee said firmly and walked away from the door.

Seconds later, a shotgun blast shattered the frame of her door. The door flew open. Renee screamed as Cliff stood in her doorway, sweaty with wild looking eyes, holding a shotgun. Renee tried to run pass him but he grabbed her by the hair and dragged her to the center of the floor. He pointed the barrel to her temple, and started crying. "Don't you understand? You killed him, dammit! This is your entire fault! My son would be alive had it not been for you!"

"Mom, who was it?" Donte asked from the top of the steps.

He did a double take when he saw his mother on the floor with the barrel against her temple. Donte started down the steps. Cliff turned and aimed the shotgun at him.

"Don't move young buck! I will kill you where you stand! Now go back up the steps!"

In a flash, Renee was on her feet, kicking Cliff in the groin. He buckled over cupping his private part. Renee grabbed the barrel, but he had a very tight grip on it. Donte bolted down the steps while Renee and Cliff tussled for the shotgun.

There was an explosion. Both Cliff and Renee fell to the floor. Donte stood there staring, waiting for movement. Cliff still had his finger locked to the trigger. A pool of blood quickly formed beneath them. Donte stood shock, staring in horror.

Cliff moved and Donte could see that he wasn't shot. His mother was.

"No-o-o-o…!" Donte screamed out like a stuck wild animal.

Cliff sat on the floor motionless, holding the gun in his hand which was now covered in blood. Donte knelt down by Renee and felt for a pulse. She was still alive but her pulse was faint, and she was bleeding badly from the stomach.

"I… I… I'm sorry," Cliff said softly.

Donte ran crying into the kitchen to call 911. He gave the operator the details and listened to her instructions to stop the bleeding. Before Donte could hang up, another explosion rocked the house. He dropped the phone and ran back into the living room. Cliff's body, the top of his head blown off, was on top his mother.

CHAPTER THIRTY EIGHT
BALTIMORE, MARYLAND

"What!" Darnell exclaimed. "Donte you're not making sense. Did you say mommy got shot?" Darnell yelled into the phone. Petie was standing in the backyard with Amir when he overheard Darnell. He rushed into the house and to Darnell he asked, "Who is that and what the fuck is going on?"

Darnell passed Petie the phone and ran upstairs to his room. Petie snatched the phone and said, "Who the fuck is this?"

"It's me, dad," Donte said weakly.

Petie could hear him crying on the other end.   He was immediately alarmed.

"What the fuck happened?" Petie asked, trying not to get too excited.

"Cliff shot mommy. I am at the hospital now waiting for the doctor to tell me something. She's in surgery, dad," Donte explained, before breaking down in tears.

"Cliff? That guy your mother was seeing? He shot her?" Petie asked, making sure that he understood what Donte had said. "Where he's at now?"

"He killed himself," Donte said. "It was crazy dad. He came in and then the next thing I know him and mommy was fighting for the gun and then it went off."

Petie could hear Donte talking to someone in the background and then Donte said, "When I saw that it was mommy that was bleeding I ran to call 911, and then I heard the gunshot. I took a look back and his head was off."

Darnell came running back down the stairs yelling, "I'm gonna kill that mothafucka!" In his hand he was holding a .380, and putting it in his waist.

"Donte, hold on," Petie said. He turned to Darnell "Put that shit back upstairs!" he ordered.

Petie watched Darnell walked back up the steps. He addressed Donte.

"Listen, I'm going to put Darnell on the next flight out of here. You just hold tight until he gets there. Has the doctor said anything to you yet?"

"No, they got me sitting in the waiting area," Donte replied, sounding like a boulder had landed on his shoulders. When Darnell came back downstairs Petie told him to pack a bag and get ready to go. All the commotion made Patrice wake up. She came down the steps asking, "What's going on?"

"My wife got shot," Petie answered and continued talking to Donte to keep him calm.

Patrice stood there with her hands over her mouth in disbelief. She knew and understood how Petie felt about Renee. Renee was legally still his wife. Patrice was only wifey.

"Oh my God," she said still holding her hands to her mouth.

Petie was still on the phone with Donte.

"Call me back collect on the other line. I want to call the airlines and see how soon I can get Darnell on a flight out."

"All right, dad."

Darnell came running down the steps with a backpack over his shoulders. He paced back and forth while Petie was on the phone getting flight schedules. Over his shoulder Petie told Patrice, "Call Chaos and tell him to get over here now."

"Okay, baby," she said and rushed to get the cellphone off the kitchen table.

"I'm gonna kill that nigga, dad. As soon as I find out that mom is alright— I'm going to get his ass!" Darnell was feeling nothing but rage.

"The nigga killed his self, Darnell. Just be quiet and let me handle this," Petie said.

Patrice came back into the living room and told Petie, "Chaos is on his way. I didn't tell him what happened."

The other phone in the house rang, and Patrice rushed to answer it. It was Donte calling back.

"Yes, I'll accept the charges," Patrice said into the phone.

Then she called out to Petie telling him that it was Donte. Petie wrote down flight information, Patrice tried to soothe Darnell. Darnell was pacing back and forth talking out loud, "...nigga shot my mom? He lucky he killed his self. I swear to God he's lucky... I can't believe this shit... Oh man, this shit is unbelievable." Darnell went on and on until Chaos pulled up and beeped the horn. Petie got the information for Darnell's flight and hung up.

"Come on, let's go," Petie said to Darnell.

Then he turned to Patrice and told her that he would be right back. Chaos drove to the airport at top speed after Petie told him what had happened. Darnell sat in the back of the truck worrying if his mother who he had cursed, and disrespected before leaving PA would die.

CHAPTER THIRTY NINE
VIRGINIA

Dougie sat in front of the television watching an episode of *Cops*. He was waiting to use the phone, but he had scheduled times that he could call home. He checked his watch, chilling in an oversized cushioned sofa, waiting for the time to pass. Finally, the lead agent came in the room.

"Make it short," he said, handing him the phone.

"Okay," Dougie said as he dialed his home number.

The phone rang through to the voicemail. Dougie hung up and re-dialed the number. Again there was no answer on the voicemail's automated voice telling the caller to leave a message. Dougie palmed his head in his hand and re-dialed the number. After the voicemail answering the call for the third time, Dougie was convinced that something was very wrong. There was always someone home at his house.

He called for one of the agents on duty and told him, "Uh, something's not right. No one is answering at my house and someone is always there."

The other agent took the phone from Dougie and said in a non-caring way, "Maybe they just don't want to speak to you. Did you ever think of that?"

He walked away and went back into the sitting room with the other agents. Dougie was on his feet in a minute shouting, "Did you hear what I said! Something is wrong! Please send someone to check on my family... Please."

The shouting aroused the attention of the other agents who were watching a game in the sitting room.

"What the hell is going on out here!" one of them shouted.

"My family… Something is wrong. No one is answering the phone and there's always someone home. Please, can you send someone to go and check on them?" Dougie explained.

"All right, just take it easy. Give me your address and I'll contact local authorities in your area and have them send a car over there to check it out," another one of the agents offered.

"Thank you, sir. I'm just worried about them. Something could've happened," Dougie said.

He sat back down and rocked in his seat. Something was wrong and he could feel it.

"Oh God, please no," he said, thinking the worst.

"Just relax, pal. We'll take care of it. Now what's your address?"

Dougie gave the agent his home address, and watched him go in the other room and close the door. Dougie could hear him talking and then rattling off his address. Moments later the same agent came out the room and told Dougie, "I contacted the locals, and they will send a squad car over there to check on things. You just relax until we get word back from them."

"Okay, sir. Thank you again," Dougie said like a good little boy.

He picked up the remote control, and turned on the news channel. For some reason he thought he would see something about his family on the news. He was scared for them knowing that if Petie found out he was working with the feds, his family would be sitting ducks.

The phone rang nearly an hour later. Agent Ward answered immediately after he recognized the number. It was the police station in South Carolina calling him back.

"Agent Ward speaking."

"Yeah this is Detective Rollins returning your call. We got eight bodies and a dog at that address that you requested. The coroner is on his way, we got the house sealed, and we're waiting for crime scene techs to arrive," the detective informed the federal agent.

"Jesus... A fucking blood bath is what it sounds like," Agent Ward replied.

He had the phone on speaker so his colleagues could hear the important call.

"How did you get wind of this?" Detective Rollins asked.

"We got a witness in protection, and he couldn't reach his family. When he really started freakin' panic, then... Turns out he was right about his hunch. He should've played lotto."

"So you got a lead on who is responsible for this?" Detective Rollins asked.

Before Agent Ward could answer, one of the other agents shook his head signaling no to him.

"At this time we're not looking at anyone in particular," Agent Ward replied lying.

This was their case and if they could tie Petie to the murders then the feds would not turn over any leads to the locals.

"All right then if you got any leads that will help my department in this case just give me a call," Detective Rollins said.

"Okay will do, detective. Just keep me informed," Agent Ward said and then disconnected the call. He looked over at his team and said, "Whaddya think we should do about this guys? Should we tell him?"

The room fell completely silent for a few seconds until one of them said, "I think we should tell him. That's not the kind of thing that you hold back from somebody. Poor guy has a right to know that his fucking family has been slaughtered."

Another agent asked, "Who is going to do the honors?"

Agent Ward stood up and said, "I will."

He walked into the living room where Dougie was sitting watching *Family Guy* on television. Dougie looked at him and anxiously said, "Did you find out anything?"

With a somber face Agent Ward responded, "It's never easy telling someone what I have to tell you, Doug."

Dougie jumped to his feet, shaking his head back and forth saying, "No, no, please don't tell me. Please, oh God please don't tell me that."

Agent Ward told Dougie about his family being found dead. Dougie dropped to his knees and cried into the carpet.

CHAPTER FORTY
NEW YORK

Will and Kalif pulled up in front of the apartment building on 151st Street. Will turned off the engine and said, "Here we are."

They got out of the car and went inside the building's vestibule. Will took his keys out of his pocket, and opened the door. He and Kalif entered the building, walked to the second floor. They went to the last apartment at the end of the hall.

Will opened the apartment door and hit the light switch. The hallway was long and carpeted with multi-color prints of beige and brown. Kalif stepped in and closed the door behind them.

"I like it already," Kalif said to Will as they walked down the hallway.

At the end of the hall was a kitchen and then to the left were the living room and a bedroom.

"All you gotta do is get some dishes, pots, pans you know little stuff," Will informed Kalif as they walked through the apartment.

The apartment had belonged to an employee who once worked at one of Share's restaurants. He had to return to Africa for a family emergency. After being gone for two months, he called and told Share that he would not be returning to the states. He had no family in New York to take care of his apartment that had a three year lease, so he told Share that she could have the apartment.

Will decided that it would be good for Kalif, especially since Stephanie kept telling Derek that Kalif was creepy. Derek not knowing what to do and he did not want to throw his friend out decided he would help Kalif with the rent for couple months until Kalif got on his feet.

"Yeah I like this," Kalif said, looking around the apartment that was now his.

He opened the closets and checked the bathroom all while smiling that he had his own place. Kalif turned to Will and gave him a pound for helping him out.

"Good looking out on everything my dude. I owe you the world," Kalif said, smiling.

"Now you just gotta get a job so you can pay this rent. The gas and electricity are included. So you know what you gotta do," Will said, meaning Kalif better get a job and do it quickly.

"Yeah, yeah no doubt, even if I gotta get out there, and sling a couple packs. You know I'm gonna maintain the rent," Kalif replied seriously.

"You might have to clean out the refrigerator, and buy some food. Other than that you are good money. I gotta get out of here, and go check on the midtown store. Call me later if anything," Will said, walking to the door. He took the keys off of the ring and passed them to Kalif.

"All right my dude, I'll holla at you later," Kalif said, closing the door behind him.

He walked back down the hall to the kitchen and opened the refrigerator. He took out the shelves and put them in the sink to soak. Kalif looked around the kitchen, realizing that he did not have anything to clean with. He walked into the living room and looked around for something to write with. Noting that he had no food, no cleaning supplies, and no cosmetics Kalif said, "Damn, let me go to the store now before I get comfy."

After cleaning and disinfecting his new apartment, Kalif went to the kitchen, and put a Hungry Man dinner in the microwave. He had done some food shopping then stopped at the discount store to get miscellaneous items for the apartment. Kalif put a DVD in the player, and waited for the microwave to signal that his food was done.

The guy that used to live there had a good selection of movies and porno DVDs. Kalif thought that he must have been one of them thugged out Africans. The microwave beeped and Kalif went into the kitchen and took his food out of the microwave. He sat down on the couch and ate while watching television.

After eating and feeling bored, Kalif decided to go out and get a bag of weed. He walked to Broadway and 152nd Street and got some haze from the Dominicans. Then he caught a cab to his old stomping grounds and checked on the guy that he used to score dust from.

A few cats that Kalif did not know told him that the guy was up north. "He's been locked up for almost three years," one of the guys told him.

"Yeah me too," Kalif said. "I did five locked down," Kalif offered, not mentioning that his time was served in a mental institution.

"Why what's up do you need something?" another guy asked.

"Yeah, you got some dust?" Kalif asked.

He could feel the knot in his stomach tightening just from the thought of smoking his drug of choice.

"I got it," another one said.

He signaled for Kalif to come with him in the building. They crossed the street, and went inside the building. The guy went up in a crack of the wall, and pulled out a plastic sandwich bag. He looked around before opening the bag and asked Kalif, "How many you want?"

"Gimme two fat ones," Kalif said, going into his pocket.

He pulled out forty dollars and gave it to the guy after smelling the dust, making sure it was official. Kalif took it and bounced quickly. It was hot out there, and the last thing he wanted was to get busted for buying dust. He caught a cab back to his new apartment, and hurried upstairs. Kalif could not wait to burn his blunt especially now that he had the dust to lace it.

Kalif got comfortable like he used to when he smoked. He sat down and rolled the blunt. After licking it with just the right amount of spit, he lit it, and pulled slowly. The familiar taste soothed his thirst he been dying to feel for nearly five years. Kalif was an addict who had just unleashed his addiction.

CHAPTER FORTY ONE
NEW YORK

Nearly an hour after smoking his first dust joint, Kalif was starting to see things appear in front of his face. Things that were not suppose to be there. He sat up and focused on a corner in the living room. Was something there? Kalif stared and broke into a sweat. His body was heating up as he tried to figure out what was in the corner looking at him. Kalif jumped up and started snatching his clothes off as sweat poured down him. He ran into the bathroom, and turned on the water in the shower. Sweat poured down his face as he peeped out of the bathroom feeling that someone was there watching him.

A car alarm outside started wailing, and Kalif jumped in the tub at the sound of the annoying noise. He almost slipped, and fell on the tile as the water poured down on him. He stood under the cold water and tried to focus. The bathroom felt like it was closing in on him.

He looked down and realized that he still had his socks on; black socks that were soaking wet. Kalif jumped out of the shower and ran into the bedroom. He peeped out of the bedroom to see if anyone was there. Kalif was tripping on the dust but to him it was real. Kalif grabbed the sheet off of the full sized bed, and wrapped it around his body. He was still on the lookout for the person that he had seen lurking in the corner. Kalif took his socks off, and threw them on the floor then he tippy-toed into the living room to investigate.

"Where are you?" he called out to the person he thought he had seen.

There was no one there. In Kalif's mind someone was there waiting. He would get them first. Kalif went into the kitchen and took a knife out of the drawer. He walked down the hallway toward the front door, and checked it. It was locked. Then he crept back down to the living room and that's when he saw him as clear as day— at least in his mind. Kalif rubbed his eyes to make sure that he was seeing right. Without a doubt someone was standing there in black socks. His black socks at that!

Kalif charged at him with the knife in his hand yelling, "Gimme my socks!"

The person that he was after had disappeared; just vanished.

"Oh God, no, Black Socks!" Kalif said, grabbing his head.

The room was spinning making Kalif feel like he was on a merry-go-round. He heard a noise come from inside the bedroom. Kalif put his back to the wall and slowly crept to the bedroom. There he was-Black Socks was sitting on the bed.

"What the hell?" Kalif said, staring at Black Socks.

Black Socks got up off the bed, and opened the window slowly. He looked back at Kalif, winked his eye then went out on the fire escape. Black Socks closed the window and then peeped in to look at Kalif. Kalif took a step back nearly tripping over his sneakers. He focused hoping that he was only seeing things and that there was no one on his fire escape wearing his socks.

Black Socks stood staring at Kalif like he was daring him to do something. Kalif walked slowly to the window and opened it. He stuck his head out and sure enough there was Black Socks sitting on the fire escape. Black Socks jumped off the fire escape and then looked up at Kalif and waved his hand. Kalif hung over the rail trying to see where Black Socks had gone still wearing his socks.

After being on the fire escape still wrapped in a sheet, waiting for Black Socks to come back, Kalif decided that enough was enough.

He went back in and sat on the couch waiting for Black Socks. He was going to kill his ass and then take his socks back. Kalif waited for hours for Black Socks to come back.

CHAPTER FORTY TWO
PENNSYLVANIA

Darnell's flight landed and he quickly made his way out of the airport; bumping and pushing people aside.

"Get out of my way! Will you please move!" he said, pushing his way out of Philadelphia National Airport. He jumped in a waiting taxi, and headed directly for Taylor Hospital.

When the cab arrived at the hospital, Darnell paid the taxi, and ran into the emergency room waiting area. Donte was sitting with Sonya by the door. Donte saw him and got up saying, "You got here quick. Mom is okay, she is out of surgery, but she's in critical condition. The doctor said that two of her ribs were broken, and she had some internal bleeding, but she's going to be fine."

"When can we see her?" Darnell asked.

"Now, I was waiting for you to come before I went in," Donte said.

He looked at Sonya and could see that she was uncomfortable seeing Darnell. This was her first time seeing Darnell since he had attacked her at her house.

Darnell paid her no mind and said to Donte, "Where is the doctor at now?"

"I don't know but the nurse will take us in to see mom," Donte said, walking towards the nurse's station. He looked back at Sonya and said, "I'll be right back."

The nurse on duty took them in to see Renee. Donte immediately broke down in tears seeing his mother lying there with tubes in her arms and a breathing mask over her face. Darnell approached the bed slowly not believing that he was looking at his mother. She looked so pale and fragile like she had lost forty pounds since he had last seen her. Donte went by the bedside, and took his mother's hand in his. He cried like a baby. Darnell walked to the other side of the bed and held her left hand. She felt cold. The first tear fell from his eyes as he looked down at the woman that he loved so much was overcome with guilt. Donte talked to Renee in hopes that she could hear him.

"Mom, I just want you to get better. Things are going to be so different for us, and I need you to hang in there. Sonya says don't forget you have to cook our graduation dinner, so get well soon. Darnell's here and well... he'll tell you himself."

"Hey, mom... Yeah, mom I just want you to know that I love you so much. I never meant to be a burden on you. I never meant to make you cry, and I'm sorry for all the times that I disrespected you. Please get well fast. Dad says to tell you that he loves you," Darnell said. His voice was filled with emotion.

The nurse finally came to tell them that they had to go. "You can always come back later," she said in a soothing tone.

"Nurse, I want to know...do you think my mom heard us when we were talking." Darnell asked.

"I would think so. She did not have brain damage or trauma to the brain," she smiled warmly and continued. "Keep talking to her. She can hear you."

"Thank you," the two brothers said at the same time.

They went out to the waiting area where Sonya was reading a magazine. She looked up as they approached, and for the first time she made eye contact with Darnell. Sonya immediately shifted her gaze.

"How is she doing?" she asked Donte.

"She looks pale and... Well she's going to be all right," he said.

Darnell started walking to the door, Donte and Sonya were behind him. Outside they walked the short distance home in silence. When they got to Donte's block, Sonya said, "Baby, I'm going to head home. Give me a call later." She stood on her tippy-toes and kissed Donte. "I love you," she said as she walked away.

"You don't have to leave because of me," Darnell said. His words stopped Sonya in her tracks.

"No it's not that…it's just that I figured you and Donte could use some time alone, and I don't want to be in the way," Sonya said modestly but at the same time lying.

"No don't go because my brother needs you," Darnell said.

Donte looked on. He appreciated what Darnell was trying to do. Inside the house, Darnell went upstairs to his old room and called Petie.

"Yeah dad it's me. Mommy is going to be fine. I didn't speak to the doctor but the nurse said that she will be okay," Darnell said as he gazed out the window, looking at nothing.

"How's Donte holding up?"

"He's all right, dad. He's downstairs with his girl. Do you want to speak to him?"

"No what time are you going back to the hospital?"

"The nurse told us to come back later. So after we eat then we'll take a walk back there," Darnell said, lying back on the bed.

"Call me from the hospital, okay?" Petie said.

"All right, dad," Darnell said before hanging up.

CHAPTER FORTY THREE
BALTIMORE, MARYLAND

"Do you see how quickly that shit rocked up?" Chaos said to Tennessee.

He stood over the stove with the glass pot in his hand. He was showing Tennessee how to cook cocaine properly without using too much baking soda.

"That's when you know your material is official. It should start cooking before you even put the flame to it. Soon as the baking soda hits it, it will fuzz up, and then you only need a touch of baking soda. It will cook itself," Chaos explained like a food chef.

"All right I got it," Tennessee said, looking on. The phone in his pocket rang so he gave the pot to Tennessee and told him, "Spin it like this." All while demonstrating how it should be done. He took his phone out of his pocket and answered it. "Yeah who's this?" the caller was one of his booty calls just back in town.

"Do you miss me?" she asked in a sultry tone.

"Yeah, I missed you. When did you get back?"

"About two hours ago. I had to get situated, do a little straightening up. My sister left the place a damn mess. When am I going to see you?"

"Tonight, I'll be available after eleven. Call me then and I'll come over you heard?" Chaos said, looking into the kitchen to make sure Tennessee was spinning the pot right.

"All right baby," she said and hung up.

Chaos went back into the kitchen, and looked at the rock. He took the glass pot from Tennessee, and poured cold water in it. He watched it carefully, making sure that it was ready. Chaos drained the water then rolled the rock out of the pot and onto paper towels, placed on the table. He checked his watch and said to Tennessee, "Lets' get the rest of that cooked up. My man and his people will be here shortly to get it. I want those niggas in and out. They're coming from North Carolina."

Tennessee started cooking the other hundred grams. Chaos looked on to make sure that he did not fuck it up. Then he put it on more sheets of paper towel and let it dry. Chaos looked at the two boulders that were now in rock form, and weighed them separately.

Too much crack. His peeps were coming to pick up one hundred and fifty grams. It weighed in at close to one hundred and eighty-five grams. He cut off the excess and weighed it again; this time it was right. The remainder of the crack went off to the side to be packaged in twenty bags for the street.

Chaos called Petie to check in on him. He had not heard from him in a couple of hours and was a little concerned. Chaos knew how Petie felt about his wife and he was very worried about what happened. Petie could not up and travel to PA like that because he was still wanted in New York, and PA was too close for comfort. Petie got on the phone sounding like he had just woke up.

Chaos asked him, "Are you all right my dude?"

"Yeah, I'm good," Petie said and yawned.

"What were you sleeping?"

"Yeah I had dozed off. Did the niggas show up yet?" Petie asked.

"Nah, they'll be here. When they come through I'll holla at you," Chaos said before hanging up.

He sat back and waited.

Tennessee moved around in the front of the house. Chaos wondered what he was doing. He started to inquire but decided it wasn't important. Tennessee had earned Petie's trust but Chaos still wondered about him.

Later that evening, Tennessee went to go look at an apartment. The woman told him that he could come over and look at it after she had gotten off work. He checked the address and walked up the path to a house on the corner. Before he could ring the bell, a woman came out on the porch.

"Are you here about the apartment," she asked giving Tennessee the once over.

He was immediately smitten by her beauty. She had perfect facial features; high cheekbones, oval eyes, and thick pretty lips. Tennessee stuttered, "Uh, uh yes I am."

"Come inside," she said, opening the door for him. "What's your name," she asked as they stepped inside.

"Denzel Foster," Tennessee answered, and closed the door behind them.

She extended her hand and said, "My name is Sherry, please to meet you."

"Do you have a piece of identification?" she asked, business-like.

"Yes, I do," Tennessee said, pulling out his wallet.

He took out the identification Petie made for him. A Maryland driver's license, about two hundred dollars... Passing it to her and saying, "Here you go." That was priceless.

She looked at the identification and then passed it back to Tennessee.

"Okay, and did you bring any recent paystubs?"

"Actually I work off the books, doing landscaping and carpentry," Tennessee said.

He felt bad lying to this woman. She seemed like a decent

hardworking woman who lived a simple life.

"Follow me; the apartment is in the basement. It is fully furnished and has basic cable. There is no separate entrance so I ask that there be no overnight guests. I don't want strangers walking through my house."

"I understand," Tennessee said, following her down to the basement.

The apartment was nicely furnished with second-hand items, but as soon as Tennessee stepped inside, it felt like home. The kitchen was at the front of the apartment, and the bedroom to the back. The bathroom was small and only had a shower. Tennessee liked it, and decided he would take it.

"Do you smoke cigarettes, drink or do drugs?"

"No, none of the above," Tennessee replied proudly.

"Good, now the rent is five hundred a month. There's a month's security deposit and the first month's rent," Sherry said.

Her eyes sparkled like an angel when she talked. Tennessee could feel Sherry's energy pouring off of her the moment he walked into the house.

"Okay, can I pay you now?" he asked.

"But you can't move in until tomorrow. I have to get an extra key made and write up a lease for you," she said eyeing him carefully.

Tennessee countedd out one thousand dollars and gave it to Sherry. "Here you go," he said and counted it as he passed her the ten one hundred dollar bills. Sherry recounted it and then said, "I'll be right back. Let me go and write you a receipt." She turned to go up the steps telling Tennessee, "You can turn on the water and see we have good water pressure and the closet space is good too." She went upstairs and wrote a receipt out for him and then returned with a key in her hand.

She said, passing the key to him, "This key is for the basement door. I still have to get a key made for the front door so that you can get in the house."

"Okay, thank you. So what time should I come pass tomorrow?" Tennessee asked as they walked back up the steps.

"Around this time is good," Sherry replied.

She walked Tennessee to the door and said, "Well, I'll see you tomorrow. Oh listen, if you want to start moving your stuff in, you're welcome to do so. I will be up until about nine then I'll be going to sleep."

Tennessee thought about it and then said, "No, I'll wait until tomorrow when I get off from work."

"Okay, well I'll see you tomorrow," she said, closing the front door.

Tennessee walked back to where he had parked, and got in the car. Things were looking better for him ever since he had met Petie. If it wasn't for Petie Tennessee would still be begging for change at the shopping center.

He drove back to the safe house where he had been staying and told Chaos about the apartment he had found and his new address. "It's real nice and cozy. I don't know if she lives alone, but I know she's not married."

Tennessee took a can of Pepsi from the refrigerator. Chaos sat there listening, wondering if he knew anyone on the block that Tennessee was talking about. He did not think so because the address did not sound familiar.

"Sounds good, I'm happy for you," Chaos said sincerely.

They talked for a short time about this and that until Chaos told Tennessee, '"We might have to take a trip to PA. I'm just waiting for Petie to decide what he wants to do. You feel me?"

"Yeah, I understand," Tennessee said.

Chaos got up to leave telling Tennessee, "Call me if anything. I'm out." He was off to see his booty call for some rest and relaxation.

CHAPTER FORTY FOUR
NEW YORK

"Oh god that felt so good," Lydia said and flopped back on the bed. She rubbed her fingers between her moist legs and with the other hand she twirled her nipple between her fingers. Her lover looked at her and lay down beside her. Lydia turned onto her stomach and her lover entered her slowly, letting his whole shaft deep into her pulsating walls. He rammed roughly inside Lydia. She squirmed, moving her legs against his thighs while moaning.

He covered her mouth and held her down as he took her. Lydia scratched at his face and wrestled her way from underneath him. She rolled from underneath him and fell on the floor.

"What the hell is wrong with you?" she yelled at the top of her lungs.

Her lover got off the bed and grabbed Lydia by her hair. He pushed her up against the wall and held her close, pushing himself deep inside her. Using his other hand to cover her mouth, he took what he wanted. Before he climaxed, he lifted Lydia off of her feet, pushing harder and harder. She bit his hand. His climax rose and pulsated until he ejaculated, trembling. His knees buckled under him and he dropped Lydia on the floor. She hit the floor hard and sprained her ankle.

"Ouch!" she screamed as she hit the floor. She looked up at her lover and rubbed her ankle.

"What the hell is wrong with you? Are you out of your mind?" she asked.

He laughed at her and went into the bathroom totally ignoring her. He closed the door to let the bathroom steam up and then turned to Lydia and said, "Hurry up and get dressed."

Lydia limped to the bed and sat down rubbing her ankle at the same time. She said to him, "Are you losing your mind? You practically raped me."

He looked at her with disgust and said, "Get dressed."

He went into the steamy bathroom, but could hear Lydia cursing while he let the water pulsate on his tight body. He laughed as he lathered.

Moments later she banged on the bathroom door and yelled, "I'm leaving! Don't call me anymore you fucken psycho!"

He turned the shower off, reached for a towel and dried off until he heard the hotel room door close. Then he rushed out of the bathroom and opened the hotel room door just in time to see Lydia get onto the elevator. He sat on the bed and continued to dry off all the while laughing quietly to his self. He was tired of Lydia anyway. Especially when he had found out that she sniffed cocaine. Andre hated women who did drugs.

Bobby stared in disbelief as Lydia limped out of the hotel. He had to look twice to make sure that it was her. Her hair was a mess, and it looked like her skirt was on backwards. She had gotten dressed in a hurry.

"What the hell happened to you?" he said quietly snapping pictures.

Lydia sped out of the parking space, almost running into a pedestrian, and cutting off a cab. He followed her onto the expressway, staying a few cars behind her. She was pushing seventy miles an hour. She was definitely in a hurry.

He called Ladelle and told him that he was following her and it looked like she was headed home. Ladelle asked, "Can you stay with her for the rest of the day?"

"Yeah, I can stay with her for a couple more hours. I'll back off and let Adam pick up if she goes to the restaurant," Bobby said.

"Alright, I'm at the restaurant," Ladelle agreed.

Bobby stuck with Lydia until she surprised him and made a stop uptown. Bobbie stayed in the car watching.

Lydia pulled up to a corner and got out. She walked across the street, and went inside a spot on Amsterdam Avenue known for crack and cocaine. She did not know that pictures were being taken of her every step. A few minutes later she came out, got back into her car and pulled away. Bobby knew the area very well. There was no need to look at his watch. He knew what time it was. Lydia just copped something. He did not know which one she had just scored.

"My, my, my you are a busy woman, aren't you...?" Bobby smiled, following her.

He quickly called Ladelle and said, "Your wife just scored something from a building on Amsterdam Ave. and 143rd Street. I'm on her now. I think she's headed home for real this time."

"Stay with her, Bobbie," Ladelle said.

"I will," Bobbie said before hanging up.

Two hours later, Lydia came out of her apartment building and got into her car. She sat behind the wheel for a short while before pulling off into traffic. Bobbie was one car behind her as she drove recklessly heading towards the restaurant. He could tell where she was going by the route she was driving. He called Ladelle and said, "She is coming your way. I'm going to put Adam on her for a few hours. Is that okay with you?"

"Yeah, that will be fine. I'll speak to you tomorrow," Ladelle said, sounding exhausted.

Poor guy, Bobby thought, hanging up. He followed Lydia to the restaurant and parked across the street waiting for Adam to pick up his tail before leaving. Lydia sat in the car for a while. She made a phone call then sashayed into the restaurant on top of the world. Ladelle was in the front of the restaurant when Lydia arrived.

Nadirah was seated at a table in the back by herself. Ladelle wanted to see if Lydia acknowledged Nadirah when she came in. He was not going to let them set him up. When Lydia entered, Ladelle was behind the counter acting as if he did not see her. She made her way to several tables, greeting patrons dinning on soul food. Ladelle noticed that Lydia breezed right pass Nadirah's table without stopping. The two women did not even make eye contact.

While Lydia continued making her way around the restaurant, Ladelle went downstairs. He sat behind the computer, looking busy. He could hear Lydia's heels on the steps as she made her way downstairs to the office. She walked up behind Ladelle and kissed him on the back of his neck. His skin crawled. He hated her touch. He wanted to turn around and tell her that he knew her dirty secret. Stop this lovey-dovey shit. Instead he said, "How was your day?"

He turned to face the woman that he had loved so much but now despised.

"It was okay," she said and sat at her desk. "I hope tonight will be better," Lydia said, winking.

He walked up the steps without responding.

CHAPTER FORTY FIVE
NEW YORK

Share ran through the hospital doors when she got the call from the doctor. He told her Venus had opened her eyes several times and was responding to the doctor's questions. Share pushed the elevator button anxiously waiting for one of the six elevators to arrive on the main floor.

When she entered Venus' room, her friend was sitting up in bed eating ice cream. Tears streamed down Share's face as she hugged her best friend. Venus was crying too as they hugged while the nurse looked on smiling. Share pulled away from Venus.

"I've been holding my breath for the day that you would open your eyes and come back to me. I love you so much, girl..." Share said, breaking down in tears again.

Venus hugged her best friend and buried her head in Share's shoulder and cried. Share pulled away and in a joking way she said, "Girl your hair is a mess."

"Well, what do you expect? I have been in a coma for weeks," Venus said, touching her hair. Then she got serious, adding, "Where is he at? In jail I hope."

"Do you remember what happened that night?" Share asked her. She pulled up the hospital chair and sat at Venus' bedside.

"Yeah, I remember up until when he pushed me and then I don't know what happened after that," Venus said.

She was trying to concentrate so she could remember what had happened but it wouldn't come to her.

"Well let me start from the beginning and tell you what's been going on," Share said. She adjusted herself in the chair and started out with, "First, I put his ass out and then I went to the precinct…"

Kalif sat at the table playing Dominoes with Derek and Will. He could not concentrate on the game because he was anxious to go home and smoke a bag of dust. He had concluded that the only reason why he had tripped the other night was because he had smoked too fast.

After finishing the last game, Kalif got up from the table saying that he was going to use the bathroom. His stomach was tight with that familiar knot when he was pre-occupied with smoking dust.

"Hurry up, nigga. Don't try to hide in the bathroom now because you're losing," Derek said jokingly.

"Nigga please I ain't losing," Kalif shot back, closing the bathroom door.

He sat on the toilet and took the bag of dust out of his pocket and smelled it. Dust had a strong smell even in the bag. After flushing the toilet, he went back into the living room, and sat back at the table. Before they could get the next game started, Kalif said, "I gotta go. I am expecting company in a little while and I wanna be home when she gets there."

"Oh you got a booty call coming over?" Will smiled.

"Yeah, sump'n like that. This new chick I met the other day says she wants to cook dinner for me," Kalif lied.

"All right, my dude you know we're not going to hold you up. We know you are still trying to catch up on all the pussy you missed doing that five," Derek said, putting the Dominos down.

Kalif got up and put on his hoodie and gave his peeps a pound then bounced. He jumped in a cab outside of the building and gave his address telling the cabbie, "Get me there quickly. I have an emergency."

He stopped at the store for a grape blunt and cigarettes before going upstairs. Kalif ran up the stairs, two at a time, to his apartment. Kalif sat at the table, and rolled his blunt laced with dust then burned it. He sat back and closed his eyes while feeling the high set in. Puffing, he let the blunt course through his mind.

His skin started crawling. He felt his body temperature rising. Kalif tried to remain calm. Then he heard noise coming from inside the bedroom. He opened his eyes for a quick second thinking that he was going to see someone. After a few seconds he heard it again. This time it sounded like someone was calling his name. Kalif opened his eyes again and got up off of the couch to check it out. He tried to extinguish the flame on the blunt, but it wouldn't go out. Leaving it burning on the edge of the window sill, Kalif walked to the bedroom and stood in the doorway, inspecting the room from a distance.

No one was there so he went to go back into the living room and that's when he heard it again. Kalif stopped in his tracks and turned back toward the empty bedroom.

"Who the fuck is that?" he asked, bending down to look under the bed.

He stood up and went to go look in the closet. He tried to open the closet door but it wouldn't open. Someone was in there holding the door from the other side.

"What the hell?" Kalif said out loud, pulling on the doorknob trying to get it to turn.

Whoever it was in there was very strong, but Kalif wanted them out of his closet. He started kicking on the door and banging on it. Kalif kicked the door so hard, the frame cracked. He was now able to open the closet door and when he did, someone ran out of the closet.

"What the fuck!" Kalif yelled, jumping against the wall.

He stood back so he could see where the person had went but he couldn't see him. Kalif took his switchblade out of his pocket, and slowly made his way to the living room, warning the imaginary person, "I have a knife and I will cut you. Now get the fuck out of my house!"

Kalif looked into the kitchen and did not see anyone there. He leaned against the wall and said, "Calm down, take it easy. There is nobody here," he smiled confidently.

Kalif went back into the living room, retrieve the burning blunt and sat down on the couch. He examined his blunt then smoked it. All the while whispering that his tripping had nothing to do with the drug, but the way he smoked it. In denial for sure, he inhaled very deeply.

CHAPTER FORTY SIX
BALTIMORE, MARYLAND

"I think it's time, Petie", Patrice said, taking deep breaths and holding her stomach.

"Time for what; I hope that you don't mean what I think you do?" Petie asked looking at her with wide eyes. Patrice could hear the panic in his voice.

She chuckled and then said, "Time for the baby. She's ready to come out." A sharp pain made her double over and grab onto the bed.

"Oh shit!" Petie exclaimed. She was early; her due date was still three weeks away. What the hell was this about?

Patrice walked slowly heading downstairs telling Petie, "We have to go, baby. My contractions are ten minutes apart."

She slowly walked down the steps with a nervous Petie trailing behind her. He ran past her on the steps and opened the back door. Petie opened the truck door and helped Patrice inside. He jumped behind the wheel, and sped out of his driveway en route to the hospital. Patrice was on the phone calling her doctor's office, telling them that she was in labor and that she was on her way in.

Petie ran two red lights and sped into the emergency room parking lot. He jumped out of the truck and ran into the emergency room yelling, "My wife is in labor. Somebody get a fucken doctor!"

Two nurses ran outside with him, while a third grabbed a wheelchair, and pushed it out the double doors. Patrice was holding her stomach as they helped her into the wheelchair. She was quickly pushed inside and taken to the emergency room, and her vitals checked. Her blood pressure was a high and her pulse was accelerated. She was given narcotics to ease the pain, while the doctor on duty immediately ordered a sonogram after she was manually examined. She was three centimeters.

They brought her to a private room, and gave Patrice a sonogram. Petie paced back and forth. He knew something was wrong from the doctor's response after checking Patrice. The sonogram confirmed that the umbilical cord was wrapped around the baby's neck. Patrice looked over at the monitor and said, "Oh my God".

Her doctor arrived just as they were wheeling her into the operating room for an emergency caesarean section.

Petie shouted at the medical team, "What the hell is going on? Somebody better tell me what the fuck is going on!"

"Sir, you have to stand back. We cannot let you inside if you don't calm down," one of the nurses said.

Patrice was being prepped for surgery and outside of the operating room she could hear Petie raising hell. They gave her an epidural shot and the doctor was ready to open her up. Petie eventually calmed down enough for the nurses to allow him into the operating room. The anxious new dad was putting on scrubs and a mask when the doctor made the first incision to deliver the baby. Petie stood looking on and ten minutes later his baby girl was delivered.

Because of the lack of oxygen her color was a purplish-blue. The newborn was rushed to intensive care, and put on an oxygen tank to help her breathing. The doctor walked with Petie to intensive care. Petie looked through the thick glass, and stared at his first daughter with tears in his eyes.

Petie stared at his daughter for nearly an hour and then he went to Patrice's room where she was recovering. He bent down and kissed her saying, "I love you, baby."

"I love you too," she said wincing at the pain as she shifted in the bed.

Petie called Chaos and asked him to pick Amir up from school and stay with him until tomorrow.

"No doubt I got you my man," Chaos said. "How much did the baby weigh?" he asked.

Petie said, "Five pounds and four ounces. She is on an oxygen tank until she can breathe on her own. Stupid ass doctor almost killed my daughter. Dumb ass Pakistani didn't even know the cord was wrapped around her neck. You know I'll be paying him a visit soon as my daughter comes home."

Petie stayed with Patrice for the rest of the night then he left the following morning to pick up Amir. The following morning when Petie and Amir arrived at the hospital, he could hear Patrice screaming and crying.

"No! No! Not my baby! What the fuck you mean she died!"

Petie ran down the hall to her room. Patrice was screaming and yelling at the medical staff. Petie quickly walked into the room, and pushed them out of his way demanding, "What the fuck happened?"

Patrice was yelling, "They killed my baby! How the fuck you telling me that she had died from eating her own stool! No-o-o!" she yelled and screamed.

Petie looked at the doctors and the rest of the medical staff that were in the room with cold eyes filled with hate. All the commotion made Amir cry. Patrice picked up her food tray and threw it at them yelling, "Y'all better get my baby! Somebody better tell me something goddammit!"

The doctor approached Petie. "Where's my fucken daughter!" he shouted.

"Sir, we are terribly sorry for what has happened. We regret to tell you that your daughter passed away in her sleep. The hospital is doing everything to find out how your daughter suffocated on her stool sometime early this morning. We did everything to resuscitate her," the doctor calmly explained.

Petie went ballistic. He pushed one of the doctors then went to Patrice and tried to calm her, but she was not having it. She pushed him backwards and started punching him out of frustration. Petie grabbed Patrice and in her ear he assured her, "I'll take care of it, just calm down, ma. I'll take care of it."

He called Chaos, telling him to come and get Amir.

"Is everything all right?" Chaos asked, hearing the emotion in his partner's voice.

"These faggots killed my daughter. Just get here and take Amir I'll explain to you later," Petie said trying to contain his emotion. The last thing he needed was to get arrested and fingerprinted.

"I'll be right there," Chaos said full of concern.

●HAPTER ᖴ●RTY ᔕEVEN
ᑎEW Y●RK

Andre sat in the second row and waited to be called. He was in court to enter a plea of 'not guilty'. He had no idea that Venus was out of the coma, and was expected in court today. Share could not wait to see Andre's face when he found out that Venus was okay.

Share and Venus entered the courtroom with the D.A.'s. assistant behind them. She said to them, "Have a seat and I will let the D.A. know that you are present. Hopefully we can get this case called and on its way."

"I hope so, because my sister does not need to be stressed anymore," Share said.

The assistant walked to the front of the courtroom, and spoke quietly into the D.A.'s. ears. He turned around briefly and then spoke to the assistant. Moments later Andre's docket number and name were called. He stood tall and straightened out his tie before walking to the front with long, confident steps. He stood behind the defendant's table with his lawyer and talked briefly with him.

The D.A. started out with, "Your Honor I would like to make the court aware that the victim is present today. She has come out of the coma and her medical team has deemed her to be present for today's session." He stopped and looked over at Andre and his attorney.

Both of them had confusion on their faces as if they did not understand what had just been said. Andre looked around until his gaze fell on Venus. She waved at him and smiled with confidence. He turned his face and said something to his lawyer.

His lawyer said, "Um, your Honor we are not here for pre-trial hearings, so it makes the court no difference if the victim is present. My client is simply entering a plea this morning so the victim being present should have no impact on the court."

The well paid lawyer down played Venus' presence like it was nothing. The D.A. immediately shot back with, "Your Honor, the victim's presence today has a great impact on the court. This is a domestic violence and assault case. The defendant beat the victim into a coma nearly killing her…"

He was cut off by Andre's lawyer shouting, "Your honor if my client was indeed trying to kill the victim then he would be charged with attempted murder-with which I'd like to remind the court that he is not."

The judge interrupted saying, "I think it is the court's decision to determine whether or not the victim being present is pertinent or not, and in this case it is. Counselor, I don't need you to remind the court what your client is being charged with…I am well aware of the charges," she said setting Andre's lawyer straight.

"Now is your client ready to enter a plea?" she asked looking down on the lawyer over her gold rimmed glasses.

The lawyer straightened his tie and said, "Yes, we are…not guilty."

She said, "Let the record show that the defendant has entered a plea of 'not guilty'."

She then set the next court date for four weeks and called the next case. Everyone filed out of the courtroom at the same time. In the hallway, Venus and Share made their way to the elevators after talking briefly with the D.A. Andre talked with his lawyer all the while keeping an eye on Venus and Share, trying to hear what they were saying.

The elevator arrived and the two women got on. Andre

rushed to catch it before the door closed. He stood off to the side, glaring at them as they rode down to the main floor. He stood in front of them blocking their path outside the courthouse. He finally said to Share, "Why are you interfering? Have you nothing else better to do with your time?"

Share said, "I don't have to explain anything to you. You piece of shit! And yes I have a lot of better things to do with my time, but I'd rather watch you get sentenced."

Venus added, "You don't have the right to question her about anything you prick. Now get out of our way before I go call the police, and tell them you're harassing us."

Andre stared at them with contempt then said to Share, "You really should be careful considering that you're sick and all. You're going to lose T-cells hating on me."

"But I bet that I will outlive you. Now, if you're looking for a fight then let's go. And if not you can get out of our way and go back to your little hotel room and count your days as a free man."

"Get the hell out of our way!" Venus shouted.

Onlookers stared at them. Andre smiled and moved to the side, letting them pass. Share spit at his feet as they walked away saying, "Coward, that's what you are."

Andre walked to the train station and headed back to the hotel with vengeance on his mind.

Bobby called Ladelle, clearly excited telling him, "Brother you're gonna love what I've got for you."

"I hope so," Ladelle said.

"I was able to meet with the woman who owns the house on

Riverdale and I gotta tell you, she's a hot one. Now I made it seem like I was new to the neighborhood, and I was able to get in her house for…well let's just say long enough to stash two mini-camcorders-one in the bedroom, and the other in the living room."

Ladelle beamed, "Oh that's great. She doesn't have any idea that they are there does she?"

"Of course not," Bobbie said confidently.

"Okay, Bobbie let me know everything," Ladelle said.

"I'll do better than that. I'll let you see everything. I have a date with her next week and that's when I'll grab the camcorder. Now, she has not been back to the hotel in about four days, but I still got Adam on her," Bobby informed Ladelle.

"Good, keep me posted," Ladelle said.

He hung up and leaned back in his chair. Everything was falling into place just like Ladelle hoped. The courts would definitely give him custody of Ladir when the time came for him to go to court. He sat back wondering what part Nadirah played in all of this.

CHAPTER FORTY EIGHT
SOUTH CAROLINA

Dougie arrived at the funeral home. He sat in the first row with his aunts, uncles, and cousins who had traveled from New Orleans. The pastor started the service talking about how good the family was. How their deaths were senseless and violent. The funeral home was large enough to hold eight caskets, and an array of flowers. Photographs of Dougie's family were placed above each of the caskets.

The service was long and sad. People kept getting up and speaking about how close the family was, and how they always offered a helping hand when needed. Women were crying while the men did their best to comfort them in their time of loss. Dougie came from a large family, and the funeral home was packed to the back. There was a long line of family members waiting to view the bodies. It was a very sad day. No dry eyes for all that had attended.

When Dougie was about to leave the funeral home, he was approached by an old childhood friend. Dougie looked up and said, "Thank you for coming, you know you were always like family to us."

The friend said, "Yeah, I'm sorry for what happened. I went crazy when I heard about it, and then they had it on the news for days straight."

"Yeah, I know," Dougie said giving his friend a hug.

The friend asked, "So where are you staying out now? The hood hasn't seen you in months."

Dougie looked around before saying, "I've been in Virginia trying to beat this case. But now since these niggas killed my family, I'm taking them down big time."

"Oh yeah I don't blame you, man. That was fucked up when I had heard about what had happened. The hood was wondering where you had dipped off to. Niggas said that you were locked up or something," the friend said.

"Nah, I'm not doing time for them niggas. Fuck them especially now after what they did," Dougie said and looked back at his family lying in caskets all because of him. He heard his name being called and looked back to see that a female agent was motioning for him to come; it was time to go.

The family friend looked over at the agent and asked, "Who's that?"

"A friend of mine, she came along to give me support," Dougie said.

"Oh, you fucking with white chicks now?" the friend asked looking at the short, blonde haired agent who looked more like a secretary.

"Nah, she's just a friend," Dougie said, looking back at her.

He told his friend that he would see him later. The friend reached out to give Dougie another hug and said, "Take care of yourself and keep in touch."

Dougie exited out to the back and then walked across the street with the agent and got into a black Range Rover.

The childhood friend watched the Rover pull away from the curb and then he took his Blackberry out of his pocket. He dialed a speed dial number and waited for it to be answered. The caller answered on the second ring saying, "Talk to me."

"Petie it's me. He just left and got into a Range Rover with some white chick. I couldn't see who was driving but I know it was them. He said he's staying in Virginia but he didn't say where," the childhood friend said.

"Oh yeah in VA, huh? What else did he say?"

"He said he was going all out and that he knows what time it is as far as his family is concerned."

"Yeah, all right good looking out," Petie said and clicked off.

He had heard enough from the same person who had given him Dougie's home address. He also supplied the car and guns. The friend closed his phone and walked back into the funeral home to talk with the family that trusted him. He wanted to find out exactly where Dougie was staying. One of the family members would tell him. After all he was like family.

Back at the house where Dougie was staying, the feds questioned him about everything he knew about Petie. They wanted to tie Petie to the murders but couldn't. He was the person they identified as a person of interest.

"After I tell y'all everything what are y'all going to do about keeping the rest of my family safe? Those niggas killed my son; he was only three years old," Dougie said, covering his face with trembling hands.

"We'll have surveillance on your grandparents house, and if need be we'll put them in safe houses. Don't worry we're going to get him, but we need to know everything about him that there is to know," the senior agent said.

Dougie wiped his face and started out with, "Well all I know is that his name is Petie. I do know that he's from New York…"

ƆHAPTER ꟻORTY ᴎINE
ꟼENNSYLᴠANIA

Donte and Darnell waited for Renee to open her eyes. She already did, and had dozed off. The doctor called Donte and told him, "Your mother is going in and out of consciousness. She's asking for you."

He dropped the phone. Donte and Darnell rushed to the hospital. Darnell sat in the corner and stared at his mother wondering what her reaction would be when she saw him. Donte pulled up a chair by her bed and held her hand rubbing it saying, "Mom, can you hear me? Mom....talk to me mom; I need to hear your voice."

Darnell stood up when he saw Renee's eyes flutter. He would do anything to hear his mother yell at him. Darnell stood on the other side of the bed and held his mother's hand. Her eyes opened slowly then closed again. She was weak and groggy from the drugs.

Filled with hope Donte said, "Mom...can you hear me?"

Renee squeezed his hand. She wanted to say something, but could not get it out. Darnell's eyes watered and he kissed his mother on the forehead.

"Talk to us mom, please," Darnell said choking up.

Her eyes fluttered again. Then slowly she opened them. Both of the brothers' faces lit up in a bright smile. Renee focused and glanced at her sons' beaming faces. She smiled and simultaneously squeezed both their hands. She tried to sit up. Darnell held her backside and Donte propped up the pillow.

"Are you in pain, mom?" Darnell asked studying her.

"No, but I need some water," she said weakly.

Darnell looked around for a water pitcher and there was none so he went out into the hallway and told the nurse, "My mother is awake and she needs some water."

The nurse asked, "Is that Renee Mickens' room?"

"Yes, that's her room," Darnell replied.

"I'll be right there."

Darnell waited until the nurse was finished. Renee was still sitting up in bed talking to Donte. Darnell could tell that his mother was weak. She looked pale and thinner. He wanted to beat the shit out of somebody-anybody for doing this to his mother.

He poured her a cup of water and watched her drink it down like she had never had water before. Darnell poured her two more cups. The doctor arrived and took Renee's vitals and then said to the brothers, "Your mother still needs rest, so don't tire her out. I'll be back to check on her again when I make my rounds."

Darnell liked the doctor because he seemed like he really cared how Renee was coming along. He looked at Renee and started crying saying, "Mom, I am so sorry for the way I acted. I swear I'll never treat you like that again."

He broke down and cried like he had never cried before.

"Yeah, dad she looks pale and weak. She looks skinnier too. We stayed until the doctor gave her some medicine and then she went back to sleep. We are going back in a few hours to spend the night with her," Darnell told Petie.

"When you get back there call me so I can speak to her," Pete stated.

"Okay dad I will," Darnell said and hung up.

He sat in front of the television staring into the blank screen. Donte came into the living room asking, "Do you wanna eat something before we go back?"

"Nah, I'm not hungry my stomach don't feel too good," Darnell said. "I really want to go see that niggas son and beat the shit out of him," Darnell said talking about Cliff's son.

"One of them killed himself in prison. That's how all this mess started and then Cliff blamed mommy for it," Donte said. He had never really had a chance to tell Darnell the entire story.

Donte finished with, "He had stole a car and mommy seen it but she didn't know it was Cliff's son until they arrested him. So, she had to go to court and then he went to jail. I don't know what happened but he hung his self and Cliff kept coming here harassing mommy saying that it was her fault."

"So what happened that day?" Darnell asked wanting to know everything.

Donte said, "It was crazy and it happened so fast...."

Back at the hospital, the two brothers arrived and could hear Renee talking to two men as they approached the open door. Darnell went in first. There were two detectives standing at the bed, asking Renee questions. This was the first interview since the shooting.

The two of them looked back when the brothers entered the room.

"These are my sons," Renee said.

She told them how Cliff had called and then she let him in not thinking that he would try to kill her. "We argued and the next thing I know he had a shotgun in his hand. I struggled with it and it went off. The next thing you know I woke up here."

One asked several more questions while the other took notes.

"Okay, well I guess that will be all. Thank you for your time," the detectives said before leaving.

Darnell kissed his mother on the forehead and asked, "How are you feeling?"

"I feel a little better than earlier. I am just constantly thirsty," Renee answered. Donte poured some water in the cup for his mother and passed it to her.

"Dad wants to speak to you," Darnell said.

"I have my phone so we can call him," Donte offered, pulling his cell phone out of his pocket.

"Call him so I can talk to him before they bring my dinner," Renee said.

Donte dialed Petie's number. He passed the phone to his mother. Petie and Renee talked for nearly an hour until an unexpected visitor knocked on the door and the let his self in. He walked in carrying flowers and card.

"How are you doing Miss Renee?"

Donte jumped to his feet immediately and said, "Get out of here. You have some nerve coming here."

Darnell had no idea who this person was but from his brother's reaction, whoever it was had no right being here.

"Who is he?" Darnell asked Donte as he too got to his feet.

"This is Chris, Cliff's oldest son," Donte said, pointing at him like he was an intruder.

"What the fuck are you doing here?" Darnell asked in a

threatening way.

Cliff's son looked at Renee and said, "I was just coming to say I'm sorry for what my father did to you, Miss Renee. I left school and got on a plane as soon as the police called me."

"Your stupid ass father almost killed my mother!" Darnell yelled, getting in his face.

"Darnell, calm down," Renee said.

"No fuck that!" Darnell said.

He pushed Chris to the wall and punched him in the gut. The flowers and card fell. Chris doubled over, coughing and grabbing his stomach. Darnell hit him again. This time they hit the floor. Chris curled up in a fetal position. Donte grabbed Darnell. Renee was trying to get out of the bed when the nurse entered the room asking, "Is everything okay in here?"

She saw Renee trying to get out of bed and rushed over to her saying, "Miss, be careful you're going to bust your stitches."

"I'm okay, really," Renee said, wanting the helpful nurse to leave.

The boy was getting up off the floor and the nurse was leaving the room. He stood up and Donte said, "Look, I think you should just leave."

From the bed Renee said, "Chris thank you for coming but now is not the right time. I think you should go."

Chris nodded, bending to pick up the flowers and the card.

Darnell barked, "You heard what my mother said so leave now!"

Chris turned to Renee and said, "I am very sorry for what happened, I really am. I hope you get well soon, Miss Renee."

Chris walked pass Darnell thinking that he was going to hit him again, and hurried out of the room. Darnell and Donte picked up the flowers and put them in a bunch.

"I'm sorry mom, I just can't believe that nigga had the nerve to come here like everything was okay," Darnell said pacing back and forth.

"I know Darnell, but he had nothing to do with this. He doesn't even live here anymore. He goes to school in Washington and it's not his fault what his father did."

Darnell listened to his mother and nodded. She was right like always. Maybe none of this would have happened if Cliff would have seen things that way. It wasn't Renee's fault what had happened to Calvin.

Renee adjusted herself in the bed and said, "You have to realize that he's in pain too. His brother is dead and now his father. He was only coming to be respectful. He didn't deserve what you did to him, Darnell."

CHAPTER FIFTY
NEW YORK

Ladelle sat in the back of Sylvia's restaurant, and waited. He checked his watch, glancing at the entrance for the umpteenth time, wondering. The waitress came back to the table.

"Sir, are you ready to order yet?"

"No not yet, I am waiting for someone," Ladelle said.

Immediately Bobby came through the door. He strutted over to the table with a smile on his face and an envelope in his hand.

"You're going to like what I got for you, brotha. Here take a look," Bobby said, passing the manila envelope.

Ladelle took out the stack of pictures and leafed through them. He became sick looking at the photos Bobby downloaded from the digital camera, set up in Nadirah's house. Ladelle looked at the pictures one more time. Then he put them back into the envelope.

"I am so sorry you had to see these pictures but you said get you everything that I could, brotha," Bobby said, sitting back with a somber look on his face.

"So do you still have the video from it? I would like to see it," Ladelle said.

"Yeah it's in the car. It's not something that we would watch in public so let's go," Bobby said, getting out of his seat. He left ten bucks on the table and walked out.

Both of them sat in the front seat. Bobby removed a DVD camcorder out the glove compartment. He turned it on and passed it to a very anxious Ladelle.

Ladelle viewed the tape and turned his nose up in disgust. He could not even watch the whole thing. There on the screen was everything he needed for full custody. He reclined in the seat, realizing he never really knew the woman on screen at all.

Lydia was having a three some, sniffing coke, the tip of the iceberg was her fucking some guy in the ass wearing a dildo. She and Nadirah did each other most of the time, licking coke off of each other's pussy and tits. Ladelle picked up the manila envelope, got out of the car and said, "Call me tonight and I will see you tomorrow for your last payment. I have everything that I need."

Bobby called out to Ladelle, but Ladelle kept going. He understood. Bobby started his car and made a U-turn, heading back to his office.

That night, Ladelle sat in the living room, watching ESPN. Lydia was in the shower, singing like always. She sounded like she had no cares in the world. He wanted to go in there and snatch her ass out of the shower and confront her. But he would have his day in court.

Ladir was in his room sleeping when Ladelle went in there. He kissed his son on the forehead and pulled the covers up on him. Ladelle looked at his little boy sleeping soundly oblivious to the lies, manipulation and the nastiness that was right in his home. He watched him for a few seconds before closing the door.

Lydia came out of the bathroom, towel drying her hair, and standing half naked in front of Ladelle.

"Are you okay, big boy?" she asked in a seductive tone.

Ladelle gazed at her before replying.

"I will be."

"What's that suppose to mean?" Lydia asked obviously

thrown off by his answer.

Ladelle got up to leave the room before he exploded on her. Lydia followed him in the room asking, "What the hell does that suppose to mean Ladelle?" He sat on the bed and held his hands in his head; he was trying to calm down because Lydia was pushing him. "Lydia, I'm really tired and I just want to get some rest. I'm just not in the mood right now," he said as calmly as he could.

"That's the problem you're never in the mood you're never in the mood for anything lately," she said; her tone laced with bitterness.

That was the straw that broke the camel's back. Ladelle jumped up off the bed yelling, "So that gives you the right to run in an out of hotels three and four days a fucking week! That gives you the right to break up our family! Oh Lydia please...spare me with the bullshit!"

Lydia's face dropped to the floor and for the first time that Ladelle could remember she was speechless. Ladelle got in her face and said, "Now deny it. I want to hear that it's all a lie. Go ahead and tell me that I don't know what I'm talking about."

"I don't know where you're getting your information from but you are so wrong," Lydia had the nerve to say before she walked out of the room. Ladelle wanted to choke her and throw her ass out of his apartment.

Walking into the living room Ladelle said, "Oh I don't know what I'm talking about? You wish I didn't. I know about everything from midtown to Riverdale."

"Who the hell do you think you are?" Lydia spat at him. "You don't know a god dam thing. You wish you had a clue but you don't so don't threaten me with your assumptions."

"Assumptions...you think that I am assuming that you're

cheating? No my dear lying ass wife, I know everything because I've seen it!"

"Ladelle you don't know what the hell you're talking about," Lydia shot back.

The venom was gone as doubt was apparent in her voice. She lost a stitch and her swagger sagged.

"You wish I didn't know but I do, Lydia. I know everything and... Well let's just say this marriage is over. You already know what comes next," Ladelle said, staring her down.

He wished that it was all a lie, but the pictures were worth a thousand words.

"So what are you saying?" Lydia asked.

"You already know. Lydia, you're a smart woman. Figure it out," Ladelle said.

"Oh so you think it's going to be that easy? You think that I'm just going to kneel down, and give up without fighting you?" she asked. Her face became contorted with anger as she continued, "I'll get everything that I ask for and more. And yes, you're right this marriage is over. It was over the day Ladir was born, so if that's what you want, then so be it. You won't win I'll tell you that much."

Ladelle was poker-faced, unimpressed with her ranting and loud threats. She had no idea of the photographs that he had. He bore a sarcastic grin watching her, knowing she didn't stand a chance.

Later that night after Ladelle went to sleep Lydia called Nadirah and said, "He knows...he knows everything. I don't know how he found out but he did. He wants a divorce, Nadirah."

Nadirah yawned and said, "So what do you want me to

do?"

She really didn't care because while she was fucking Lydia, she never told Lydia that she had been trying to fuck Ladelle too. Lydia had never known that Ladelle had been at Nadirah's house.

"What do you mean, what do I want you to do? I want your help dammit! Oh forget it it's not your marriage that's in jeopardy so what do you care?"

Nadirah rolled back over to go back to sleep knowing that it was no sweat off of her back.

CHAPTER FIFTY ONE
BALTIMORE, MARYLAND

Patrice lay on the bed curled up in a fetal position. Petie stood over her and said, "Ma, I'm going to take care of this. Please I need you to pull yourself together for now."

"How the hell are you going to take care of this!" she yelled, sitting up on the bed. "Are you going to bring my baby back? Huh! Are you?"

She broke down in tears crying. Then Patrice got up in his face and said, "You kill all of them muthafuckas, daddy. I want them to suffer like we are."

Patrice had never condoned any of Petie's violence especially after Amir had been born. She wanted him to leave the life alone and start fresh. Now she wanted him to kill anything moving.

Chaos and Petie sat outside of the hospital and waited for nearly two hours in a rental car. It was after one in the morning when they spotted Patrice's doctor leaving.

"There he is," Petie said, putting on gloves and pulling the skully over his face.

The doctor had no idea as he walked to his car unaware. Petie walked quickly up on the doctor, without saying a word he pumped two silenced bullets in his heart. The doctor fell slowly to the ground, clutching his chest. He looked up for a brief moment into Petie's eyes.

Chaos was behind the wheel waiting, before Petie could

close the door, he was pulling out of the parking lot. They headed to the all night Avis rental place. Sissy and Butter were waiting to return the car. They pulled up at their designated spot and changed cars.

Sissy and Butter wiped the car down with gloved hands and Petie and Chaos headed back to the spot.

Inside the car Petie said nothing. Chaos said, "I think it's time to bounce."

"Bounce…?" Petie asked. "I know you ain't trying to run out on me now," Petie said, cutting his eye at his partner.

He stopped the truck and they both remained silent for a moment. The calm was broken when Chaos glanced across the street.

"We need to hit that bank. I been telling you about that for the longest. Then we get the fuck up outta the country. Go somewhere… Where they don't have extradition laws, like St. Thomas," Chaos said.

Petie looked at Chaos. He had been telling Petie for over a year that he wanted to hit that bank across town. Sissy was tricking off with the bank manager, and she had initially brought the idea up to Chaos. Sissy and Butter were their down-for-anything-bitches, and they were 'bout it.

"Shit's closing in on us. This nigga Dougie and his rat ass… It's time to bounce, my nigga. Ain't nothing left here for us," Chaos said, looking more serious than ever.

Petie started driving again. His wrinkled brow said he was giving the matter some thought. It was time to go because shit was getting critical. Petie had been on the run for seven years. It wouldn't last forever. Petie dropped Chaos off then headed home.

Patrice was up waiting for him in the living room when he got in. Petie locked the door, and set the alarm. He sat down on the couch and said, "I got him."

"Good, now my baby can rest," Patrice said, getting up off the couch.

Petie followed her upstairs, thinking how the death of their daughter had changed her so quickly. Patrice had never been one for violence, but she was filled with vengeance since their daughter died.

Petie took a long shower, and got in the bed. Patrice had a drink in her hand as she sat up and stared at nothing. Petie looked over at her and said, "Ma, we're gonna get pass this."

Petie went to sleep thinking about what Chaos had told him earlier. He knew that they should do it. Everything good was now turning bad.

EPILOGUE

Andre copped out to five years, after his lawyer told him that it was not wise to go to trial. He had fought the case for eight months, and the judge was tired of it and said, "Get ready for pre-trial hearings, or take the time that the state is offering."

His lawyer had told him, "If we go to trial we will lose. I think it's in your best interest to cop out before the state withdrawals their offer."

Andre was mad as ever and wanted to kill his lawyer, but still had to plead guilty.

Venus was recovering from her injuries, and was more than happy to see her ex being sentenced to five years. Inside the court room Andre looked back at her with eyes filled with hate. He was handcuffed and led out of the courtroom. Share waved bye-bye to him.

Venus moved out of Share's brownstone in the Bronx, and moved into the one that she owned on 146th Street and Riverside Drive. She said that the other one had too many memories of her and Andre. She took self-defense classes, and opened a house for abused women.

Renee recovered from her injuries and was released from the hospital. She and Darnell's relationship improved tremendously. He even brought Felicia home to meet his mother. Renee like Felicia immediately and knew her son made a wise choice. She only hoped Darnell stayed on the right path.

Sonya and Donte graduated from high school and both will start college in the coming fall. Donte was on the basketball team with big hopes of becoming an NBA draft. Sonya finally forgave Darnell, and wished him well in his relationship with Felicia.

Ladelle filed for divorce and after learning about the pictures and the explicit tape, Lydia did not contest the divorce. She was awarded nothing. Ladelle gave her ten-thousand dollars, and told her to hit the road. Nadirah tried to push up on Ladelle, but he was not impressed, and told her to beat it. Petie and his team were fully aware that Dougie was trying to get them locked, detained and subdued.

That's all for now... The rest is to be continued...

WHERE
HIP-HOP
LITERATURE
BEGINS...

AUGUSTUS PUBLISHING

Augustus Publishing was created to unify minds with entertaining, hard-hitting tales from a hood near you. Hip Hop literature interprets contemporary times and connects to readers through shared language, culture and artistic expression. From street tales and erotica to coming-of age sagas, our stories are endearing, filled with drama, imagination and laced with a Hip Hop steez.

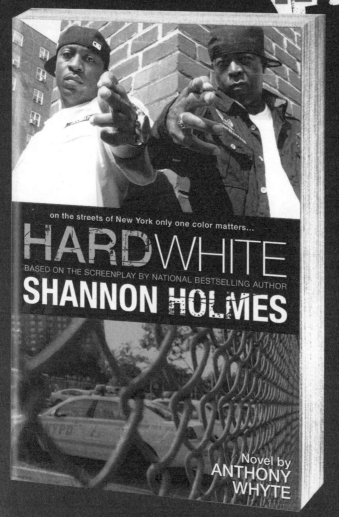

Hard White: On the street of New York only on color matters
Novel By Anthony Whyte Based on the screenplay by Shannon Holmes

The streets are pitch black...A different shade of darkness has drifted to the North Bronx neighborhood known as Edenwald. Sleepless nights, there is no escaping dishonesty, disrespect, suspicion, ignorance, hostility, treachery, violence, karma... Hard White metered out to the residents. Two, Melquan and Precious have big dreams but must overcome much in order to manifest theirs. Hard White the novel is a story of triumph and tribulations of two people's journey to make it despite the odds. Nail biting drama you won't ever forget...Once you pick it up you can't put it down. Deftly written by Anthony Whyte based on the screenplay by Shannon Holmes, the story comes at you fast, furiously offering an insight to what it takes to get off the streets. It shows a woman's unWlimited love for her man. Precious is a rider and will do it all again for her man, Melquan... His love for the street must be bloodily severed. Her love for him will melt the coldest heart...Together their lives hang precariously over the crucible of Hard White. Read the novel and see why they make the perfect couple.

$14.95 / / 9780982541531

NATIONAL BESTSELLING AUTHOR
ANTHONY WHYTE

STREET CHIĆ

A NOVEL

Street Chic
By Anthony Whyte

A new case comes across the desk of detective Sheryl Street, from the Dade county larceny squad in Miami. Pursuing the investigation she discovers that it threatens to unfold some details of her life she thought was left buried in the Washington Heights area of New York City. Her duties as detective pits her against a family that had emotionally destabilized her. Street ran away from a world she wanted nothing to do with. The murder of a friend brings her back as law and order. Surely as night time follows daylight, Street's forced into a resolve she cannot walk away from. Loyalty is tested when a deadly choice has to be made. When you read this dark and twisted novel you'll find out if allegiance to her family wins Street over. A most interesting moral conundrum exists in the dramatic tension that is Street Chic.

$14.95 / / 9780982541500

When Love Turns To Hate
By Sharron Doylee

Petie is back regulating from down south. He rides with a new ruthless partner, and they're all about making fast money. The partners mercilessly go after a shady associate who is caught in an FBI sting and threatens their road to riches. Petie and his two sons have grown apart. Renee, their mother, has to make a big decision when one of her sons wild-out. Desperately, she tries to keep her world from crumbling while holding onto what's left of her family. Venus fights for life after suffering a brutal physical attack. Share goes to great lengths to make sure her best friend's attacker stays ruined forever. Crazy entertaining and teeming with betrayal, corruption, and murder, When Love Turns To Hate is mixed with romance gone awry. The drama will leave you panting for more....

$14.95 / / 9780982541517

SMUT central
By Brandon McCalla

Markus Johnson, so mysterious he barely knows who he is. An infant left at the doorstep of an orphanage. After fleeing his refuge, he was taken in by a couple with a perverse appetite for sexual indiscretions, only to become a star in the porn industry... Dr. Nancy Adler, a shrink who gained a peculiar patient, unlike any she has ever encountered. A young African American man who faints upon sight of a woman he has never met, having flashbacks of a past he never knew existed. A past that contradicts the few things he knows about himself... Sex and lust tangled in a web so disgustingly tantalizing and demented. Something evil, something demonic... Something beyond the far reaches of a porn stars mind, peculiar to a well established shrink, leaving an old NYPD detective on the verge of solving a case that has been a dead end for years... all triggered by desires for a mysterious woman...

$14.95 // 9780982541586

Dead And Stinkin'
By Stephen Hewett

Stephen Hewett Collection brings you love as crime. Timeless folklores of adventure, heroes and heroines suffering for love. Can deep unconditional love overcome any obstacles? What is ghetto love? One time loyal friends turned merciless enemies. Humorous and powerful Dead and Stinkin' is tragic and twisted folktales from author Stephen Hewett. The Stephen Hewett Collection comes alive with 3 intensely gripping short stories of undying love, coupled with modern day lies, deceit and treachery.

$14.95 // 9780982541555

Power of the P
By James Hendricks

Erotica at its gritty best, Power of the P is the seductive story of an entrepreneur who wields his powerful status in unimaginable — and sometimes unethical — ways. This exotic ride through the underworld of sex and prostitution in the hood explores how sex is leveraged to gain advantage over friends and rivals alike, and how sometimes the white collar world and the streets aren't as different as we thought they were.

$14.95 // 9780982541579

America's Soul
By Erick S Gray

Soul has just finished his 18-month sentence for a parole violation. Still in love with his son's mother, America, he wants nothing more than for them to become a family and move on from his past. But while Soul was in prison, America's music career started blowing up and she became entangled in a rocky relationship with a new man, Kendall. Kendall is determined to keep his woman by his side, and America finds herself caught in a tug of war between the two men. Soul turns his attention to battling the street life that landed him in jail — setting up a drug program to rid the community of its tortuous meth problem — but will Soul's efforts cross his former best friend, the murderous drug kingpin Omega?

$14.95 // 9780982541548

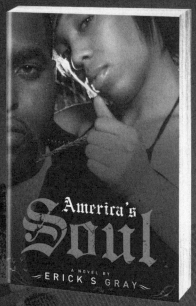

GHETTO GIRLS IV

Young Luv

ESSENCE BESTSELLING AUTHO
ANTHONY WHYTE

Ghetto Girls IV Young Luv
$14.95 // 9780979281662

Ghetto Girls
$14.95 // 0975945319

Ghetto Girls Too
$14.95 // 0975945300

Ghetto Girls 3 Soo Ho
$14.95 // 0975945351

THE BEST OF THE STREET CHRONICLES TODAY, THE **GHETTO GIRLS SERIES** IS A WONDERFULLY HYPNOTIC ADVENTURE THAT DELVES INTO THE CONVOLUTED MINDS OF CRIMINALS AND THE DARK WORLD OF POLICE CORRUPTION. YET, THERE IS SOMETHING THRILLING AND SURPRISINGLY TENDER ABOUT THIS ONGOING YOUNG-ADULT SAGA FILLED WITH MAD FLAVA.

Love and a Gangsta
author // ERICK S GRAY

This explosive sequel to **Crave All Lose All**. Soul and America were together ten years 'til Soul's incarceration for drugs. Faithfully, she waited four years for his return. Once home they find life ain't so easy anymore. America believes in holding her man down and expects Soul to be as committed. His lust for fast money rears its ugly head at the same time America's music career takes off. From shootouts, to hustling and thugging life, Soul and his man, Omega, have done it. Omega is on the come-up in the drug-game of South Jamaica, Queens. Using ties to a Mexican drug cartel, Omega has Queens in his grip. His older brother, Rahmel, was Soul's cellmate in an upstate prison. Rahmel, a man of God, tries to counsel Soul. Omega introduces New York to crystal meth. Misery loves company and on the road to the riches and spoils of the game, Omega wants the only man he can trust, Soul, with him. Love between Soul and America is tested by an unforgivable greed that leads quickly to deception and murder.

$14.95 // 9780979281648

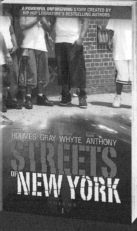

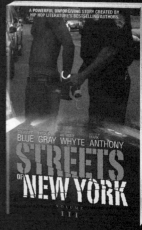

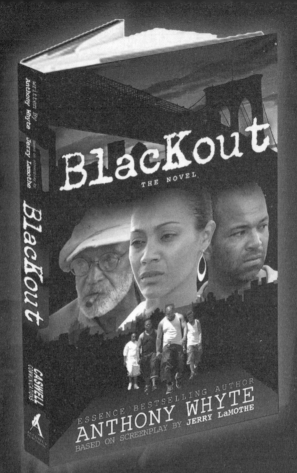

The lights went out and the mayhem began.

It's gritty in the city but hotter in Brooklyn where a small community in east Flatbush must come to grips with its greatest threat, self-destruction. August 14 and 15, 2003, the eastern section of the United States is crippled by a major shortage of electrical power, the worst in US history. Blackout, the spellbinding novel is based on the epic motion picture, directed by Jerry Lamothe. A thoroughly riveting story with delectable details of families caught in a harsh 48 hours of random violent acts, exploding in deadly conflict. There's a message in everything... even the bullet. The author vividly places characters on the stage of life and like pieces on a chess-board, expertly moves them to a tumultuous end. Voila! Checkmate, a literary triumph. Blackout is a masterpiece. This heart-stopping, page-turning drama is moving fast. Blackout is destined to become an American classic.

BASED ON SCREENPLAY BY JERRY LaMOTHE
Inspired by true events

US $14.95 CAN $20.95
ISBN 978-0-9820653-0-3

CASWELL
COMMUNICATIONS